"I can't tell you ho[...] means to us..."

"You've made my son the happiest little boy in the state of Colorado."

"He deserves all the happiness in the world." Logan paused for a moment, his gaze unwavering. "You both do."

Caitlyn stood quietly. A tear ran down her cheek.

Logan gently wiped away the tear from her face. "This is a day for smiles, not for tears."

"I know." Caitlyn shook her head. "I'm sorry, but I'm just so happy."

"So am I." Logan smiled. "I promise you, the best is yet to come."

Caitlyn nodded quickly. "You're right. I can hardly wait to see Henry's face when he meets Cooper."

Logan took Caitlyn's hand and led her outside. A cool breeze brushed his face. "I'm excited for Henry to meet Cooper too, but that wasn't exactly what I was referring to."

Caitlyn looked up. Her eyes shimmered with emotion. "I can't imagine things ever getting any better than they are at this moment..."

Weekdays, **Jill Weatherholt** works for the city of Charlotte. On the weekends, she writes contemporary stories about love, faith and forgiveness. Raised in the suburbs of Washington, DC, she now resides in North Carolina. She holds a degree in psychology from George Mason University and a paralegal studies certification from Duke University. She shares her life with her real-life hero and number one supporter. Jill loves connecting with readers at jillweatherholt.com.

Books by Jill Weatherholt

Love Inspired

Second Chance Romance
A Father for Bella
A Mother for His Twins
A Home for Her Daughter
A Dream of Family
Searching for Home

K-9 Companions

Their Inseparable Bond
Her Son's Faithful Companion

Visit the Author Profile page at LoveInspired.com.

Her Son's Faithful Companion

JILL WEATHERHOLT

PLEASE RECYCLE
THIS PRODUCT IS RECYCLABLE

Recycling programs for this product may not exist in your area.

ISBN-13: 978-1-335-59740-3

Her Son's Faithful Companion

For questions and comments about the quality of this book, please contact us at CustomerService@Harlequin.com.

Love Inspired
22 Adelaide St. West, 41st Floor
Toronto, Ontario M5H 4E3, Canada
www.LoveInspired.com

Printed in Lithuania

But as it is written, Eye hath not seen,
nor ear heard, neither have entered into the heart of
man, the things which God hath prepared for them
that love him.

—*1 Corinthians* 2:9

To Suzanne, for over fifty years of friendship and laughter.

Chapter One

Inheriting her childhood home along with a valuable piece of land might be the answer to Caitlyn Calloway's prayers. Selling the property could hold the promise of some financial relief, allowing Caitlyn to provide her son with the care he deserved. Last year's epilepsy diagnosis had buried her under a mountain of bills, pushing her months behind on the rent for their cramped Wyoming home. Selling might even free Caitlyn from the turbulent memories associated with the death of her parents, casting a shadow over her adult life.

"Let's go inside, Mom."

Caitlyn glanced at her seven-year-old son, Henry. At the rate he was growing, he'd surpass her five-foot-four-inch frame by the end of next year. His sandy-blond hair desperately needed a cut, as evidenced by the tousled wavy locks practically covering his ears. Signing his adoption papers two years earlier, after fostering Henry for a year, had been the best day of her life. Henry's kind heart and dimpled smile were the reasons she got out of bed each morning. She slid her phone from her bag to double-check the text message from the estate attorney. "The caretaker should be here soon, but we're a couple minutes early. Let's wait until he gets here before going inside." With no updates to the first text, Caitlyn tucked the phone away.

Late May thunderstorms had extended the drive from Wyoming to Bluebell Canyon, Colorado. The weather had forced them to stay overnight at a motel outside of Denver. An unexpected expense that added pressure on Caitlyn's already strained finances.

Henry's gangly jean-clad legs took the stacked stone steps of the farmhouse two at a time. At the top, he spun on his heel. "I can't believe you lived here. This house must be really old…like you." He giggled while gazing at the large two-story home with a steeply pitched roof. The painted trim underneath the gutter appeared chipped and peeling. "Cool! It's got a real fireplace—not like our fake one!" Henry pointed to the weathered red-brick chimney on the end of the house.

It was nice to see him so happy. Lately, the stress of Henry's diagnosis of epilepsy had taken a toll on Caitlyn. She felt as old as the restored eighteenth-century home she'd inherited. A place that had once provided a carefree childhood had developed into a tumultuous environment the year she'd turned seven.

"Funny guy, now come down and wait with me."

"Look!" He jumped and snatched hold of a weathered cord hanging from a cast-iron bell. Two quick pulls sparked a vivid memory of Caitlyn's mother. Ringing the bell meant dinner was on the table.

"Henry! Down here, now," she snapped.

"But I want to try this cool swing." Henry's tennis shoes whacked against the cedar porch as he sprinted toward the old two-person swing hanging from the ceiling by frayed rope. The splintered wooden seat appeared it would collapse even with the weight of a child.

"Stop! It's not safe." Caitlyn's sharp tone cut through the

air. She bolted up the stairs and toward Henry to prevent him from climbing on the rickety swing.

Henry stopped short and turned with a puzzled expression. "What's wrong? I just wanted to play on it."

Caitlyn couldn't blame Henry. As a child, she'd had many fond experiences on this porch swing. She pulled her dark brown ponytail over her shoulder, knelt and took Henry's hand in hers. "I'm sorry, sweetie, but the swing is too old and it could break if you sit on it. You might get hurt."

Henry glanced over his shoulder before turning back to his mother. "Yeah, it looks kind of old, like the rest of the house."

Caitlyn stood and guided Henry to the top step of the porch. "Let's sit."

Henry followed her lead and sat down. "Has the swing always been here?"

"Shortly after my parents were married and moved into the house, my dad built the swing for my mom. In the evening, when my dad would come in from working in the field, he liked to relax out here." Caitlyn's heart squeezed as a vivid picture of her dad crossing the field and waving filled her mind. With a pitcher of lemonade on a nearby table, Caitlyn's bare feet had swung back and forth over the wooden floor while she'd anxiously waited for her father. "When I was not much younger than you are now, in the summer, I'd always wait for him with something cold to drink. He'd climb the steps, take off his cowboy hat and always say with a smile, 'Hey there Katydid. How was your day?' before he took a seat next to me."

Henry giggled. "That's a bug! Why did he call you that?"

"Once I was old enough, my father told me when I was around two years old, I started to giggle each time we'd hear the Katydid chorus during the summer. Anyway, I'd snuggle beside him, and we would enjoy the soothing motion swinging back and forth while we watched the sun set over the Rocky Mountains. He'd tell me stories about when he was a little boy."

Sounds of a diesel engine rumbled. Caitlyn peered over her shoulder and spotted a blue extended-cab pickup truck heading down the dirt driveway. "There's the caretaker. Let's go." She pulled her hands from the back pockets of her jeans and motioned for Henry to follow her down the steps.

Adrenaline coursed through her body. In a matter of minutes, she'd be inside the home she'd run away from a month before her seventeenth birthday.

With Henry at her side, Caitlyn squinted into the bright sun and wished she hadn't forgotten her sunglasses at the motel this morning. She watched as the truck pulled around to the side of the wraparound porch.

Seconds passed before the door slammed and gravel crunched.

Caitlyn placed a hand over her eyebrows and spotted a tall, ruggedly muscular outline approaching. A stray cloud drifted across the sun, finally revealing a face. Memories flooded her mind. Her breath caught. *Logan.*

"Caitlyn?"

The crinkled brow and stunned expression proved her presence had equally surprised Logan Beckett. Surprised or not, Caitlyn clearly remembered the piercing green eyes that always remained focused on whoever was in his presence. His neatly cut black hair with flecks of gray around the temples highlighted his firm jawline. The two had met during her years on the rodeo circuit as a professional barrel racer. Logan's brother, Luke, a professional bull rider, had been a good friend to Caitlyn.

She blinked rapidly to will away the butterflies flitting in her stomach. "This is a surprise." Her voice trembled.

A slow smile that could make friends in an instant crossed his face. He tilted his head to one side, sending a shiver down Caitlyn's back. In Logan's company, she'd always had this reaction, but her desire to be the best barrel racer had kept her focus off of Logan and on the sport.

"Hi! I'm Henry. Who are you?"

"It's nice to meet you, Henry. I'm Logan. Your mother and I are old friends."

Logan moved closer and gave Caitlyn an awkward hug, pulling her closer to his broad shoulders. His six-foot-two-inch frame towered over her. He smelled nice, reminding her of the spicy nutmeg she used to make Henry's favorite pancakes. Still trying to understand Logan's presence, Caitlyn pulled away from his muscular arms and took a step back. "Are you the caretaker for this property?"

"No, I lease several hundred acres of land, but Joe Lucas has taken care of the house since the owner, Martha Williams, moved to Florida. She recently passed away and Joe has left Bluebell. I got a voice mail from him about an estate attorney needing the key to the property," Logan explained. "Did you know Martha?"

Caitlyn remained confident her parents wouldn't have chosen Martha as her guardian if they had foreseen the eventual downward spiral of her life. "She was my mother's best friend and my guardian after my parents died."

"I remember Luke mentioning the car accident. I'm sorry."

Caitlyn nodded. "It's been a long time." She turned and focused on the farmhouse. "This was my home for almost seventeen years." Following the death of her parents at seven years old, Caitlyn had no other choice than to place her trust in Martha. Years later, when Martha had brought her boyfriend into the home, Caitlyn had realized what a mistake she and her parents had made for trusting the woman. "At the time of the accident, except for me, my parents didn't have any living relatives, so they willed the home and property to Martha. Until recently, I didn't know my parents' will stipulated everything would go to me upon Martha's death, as long as I was of legal age. I haven't spoken with her since I left for Wyoming when I was a teenager."

Caitlyn forced the ugly memories of why she left into the back of her mind. "So, is Joe returning, or do you have the key?"

Henry bounced on his toes. "Yeah, I want to see my mom's old bedroom."

Logan grinned and ruffled the top of Henry's sandy-blond hair. "I don't have the key, but Joe told me where Martha stashed a spare. I'll run around back and grab it."

Caitlyn watched Logan round the corner of the porch.

"Was he in the rodeo with you, Mom?"

"No, but his brother Luke was a professional bull rider." Although she and Luke were closer in age, back then, she'd carried a secret crush on Logan.

"That's so cool! Maybe if the doctors find a cure for epilepsy, I can be a bull rider, too."

Caitlyn prayed for a cure. Since the diagnosis over a year ago, she'd tried to stay positive and encourage Henry. She never wanted Henry to feel limited. "Maybe so, sweetie. Let's go up on the porch while we wait for Mr. Beckett." Caitlyn took her son's hand and headed up the front steps. A loose board rattling underneath her foot caused her to question exactly how long Joe, the caretaker, had been out of town.

Grateful for a moment to calm her nerves after the surprise appearance by Logan, Caitlyn scanned the expansive green pasture then looked down at her son. "You like it here, don't you?"

Henry's head bobbled up and down. "If this is your house, why can't we move here?"

"Our home is in Wyoming. Plus, your friends are there." If moving to Colorado would make the pile of past-due bills waiting on her desk disappear, Caitlyn would move in a heartbeat. By summer, using the proceeds from the sale of her inheritance, Caitlyn hoped to have Henry's medical bills paid off, as well as the overdue rent to her landlord. Then she'd expand the size of the barrel racing classes she taught and extend the hours. One day, she dreamed of having schools across the state of Wyoming that offered specialized boot camps, along with private lessons. Maybe even offer an all-inclusive camp where the girls could stay for a week. Caitlyn had always believed a solid foundation was the key to excellence in the arena.

Henry struggled to sit still and squirmed on the porch step. "But if we moved here, no one would know I have epilepsy. I could have more friends. Back home, lots of the guys are afraid to play with me now."

Caitlyn rested her arm around Henry and pulled him closer. After a recent seizure he'd had at school on the playground, she'd noticed many of Henry's friends wouldn't come by the house anymore. She'd talked to some mothers who'd explained witnessing the seizure had frightened their children.

"Give them time. They'll come around."

Footsteps rustled in the grass. "Are you ready to see the inside?" Logan bounded up the steps two at a time, flashing the key.

Henry jumped from the step and followed Logan to the front door. "I am!"

Logan slipped the key into the lock and turned it.

There was no turning back. Caitlyn inhaled deeply. In the weeks leading up to the night she'd run away from home, Caitlyn had kept a close eye on her bedroom door. For more than half of her life, she'd avoided coming home, but now, for the sake of her son, she had no choice but to face her past.

"It looks old," Henry noted as he shadowed Logan inside.

Caitlyn's heart thumped in her chest when she stepped over the threshold and into the front room, or the parlor, as her mother had called it. Instantly recognizing the peeling gold wallpaper, she pressed her damp palms against her legs. Caitlyn's father had hung the paper as a birthday surprise for her mother.

Logan flipped the light switch and moved toward the front windows. "Let's bring in a little daylight. It might brighten things up a bit." He drew the curtains. Particles of dust swirled in the sunlight that came streaming through the window.

"I think it was better without the light." Caitlyn scanned the room. The once-luminous hardwood flooring was now dull and covered with black scratch marks. "When exactly did Joe leave town?"

Logan rubbed his neck. "It's kind of hard to tell. He's never had a steady job, but he goes off for long stretches in search of work as a ranch hand. I tried to help by offering him temporary jobs here and there, but he was never reliable."

Caitlyn tilted her head. "It's obvious he didn't take his job as caretaker seriously. Martha couldn't have been aware of this or she wouldn't have continued to pay him."

Logan closed the space between himself and Caitlyn. He glanced toward the kitchen where Henry had wandered, but was still in sight. He whispered, "You must know about Martha's drug and alcohol problem."

Caitlyn nodded. "Yes, but like I said, I hadn't spoken to her in years." After Caitlyn had left Colorado, she'd prayed that one day Martha would reach out to apologize. Perhaps even share if she'd overcome her addiction.

"Before she left town, my brothers and I tried to help her, but by the time she left for Florida, she was in terrible shape. It was a shame. She'd once been a gracious lady, but seemed to get mixed up with the wrong company."

When Caitlyn was around twelve, Martha had turned to alcohol following a nasty breakup. The woman her parents had entrusted to care for their daughter had morphed into a different person. "I suppose Joe and Martha both weren't too concerned about the property…that explains why the place is in much worse shape than I expected."

"Mom! Come look! There's a mouse back here," Henry shouted from the kitchen.

"Why am I not surprised?" Caitlyn scurried to the rear of the home. Loose floorboards rattled underneath her boots. Another expense.

Logan followed. "By the look of things, there's probably more than a few mice running around the place."

Shelling out money for a motel room last night was already more than Caitlyn could handle. She didn't have the funds to stay anywhere while in Bluebell, so the plan had been to remain in the house while she addressed any necessary repairs. But with mice—and anything else—creeping around the home, the dilapidated floorboards, the peeling wallpaper, and who knows what other problems, she might have to come up with another solution. But what other option was there?

"Are you sure you saw a mouse?" Caitlyn immediately

noticed the kitchen was in no better condition than the front room.

"Yeah, look over there." Henry pointed.

Logan chuckled as he looked in the critter's direction and turned to Henry. "You must live in the city in Wyoming. That's a chipmunk."

Caitlyn's shoulders relaxed. "I suppose a chipmunk is better than a mouse, right?"

"Not necessarily." Logan moved to the walk-in pantry, pulled out a broom, and headed to the door leading from the kitchen to the back porch. "These little guys might be cute, but similar to a squirrel, they can be quite destructive. If they chew on the wiring, that could create a fire hazard. Plus, they can burrow holes in the backyard. The last thing you want is to break your ankle walking around in the yard. My guess is the enormous chestnut tree along the fence line is the primary food source." He opened the door before walking over to the chipmunk, who appeared too interested in his chestnut stash in the corner to notice anyone.

What if there was already damage to the wiring? Caitlyn bit her lower lip. Electricians cost a fortune. "So, how do I keep them from coming inside the house?"

Logan used the broom and guided the critter across the kitchen floor and out onto the back porch. He closed the door and squatted. "First, I'll need to seal entry points, crevices and gaps, similar to this one." He pointed to the gaping hole at the baseboard.

Was Logan offering his services for free? She'd learned the hard way not to depend on a man. Her skills with a hammer were better than most. Caitlyn scanned the room and spotted two more holes in the kitchen. "That could be an extensive project." Visions of her bank account balance depleting played in her mind.

"Probably so, but I can get it knocked out in no time. We don't want any snakes to find their way inside."

"Cool! I always wanted a pet snake," Henry cheered.

Logan stifled a laugh.

A shiver traveled up Caitlyn's back. She could handle most creatures, but she drew the line with snakes. This wasn't good. The rooms downstairs required significant attention. Martha had left a small amount of money to cover household repairs, but not nearly enough for all the issues Caitlyn could see. Concern rolled around in her head. Caitlyn couldn't help but wonder what they'd find on the second floor…

Caitlyn was as cute as Logan remembered, with her heart-shaped face and the light brown freckles across the bridge of her pert nose. Although still petite, she'd grown up from her early competitive barrel racing days when he'd first laid eyes on her. Back then, she was barely out of her teen years. Now she could turn every man's head in a packed stadium. And she had a child.

"Do you think there are snakes in the house?" Caitlyn gnawed on her thumb while her hazel eyes shifted around the kitchen.

"It's a little early in the season, but you could have a problem this summer if I don't get the house sealed properly." Logan closed the door and returned the broom to the pantry.

"Henry and I will be long gone by then. The new owner will have to deal with any unwelcome visitors."

It surprised Logan to hear Caitlyn could so easily sell her childhood home. If he had kids, he'd love for them to grow up in the house where he'd lived as a child. Maybe her work kept her busy in Wyoming. "Do you still compete?

You were pretty good." Logan knew she had exceptional talent. He'd followed her career closely for several years. There was a time when Caitlyn Calloway had been the most successful barrel racer on the rodeo circuit.

Caitlyn laughed. "No, I retired a few years ago. The sport is for the younger generation." She reached down and rested her hands on Henry's shoulders. "These days, this guy keeps me running in circles."

Overhead, a loud thump sounded.

Logan peered up at the ceiling. "I'm not sure what that noise was, but I guess we better go check out the upstairs. It's probably nothing." Old houses often made unexplained noises.

Henry jumped up and down. "That sounded like a bear or something! Let's go see!"

Logan laughed when Caitlyn rolled her eyes. "I'll go first. I've had a little experience with bears out in the woods." He winked at Caitlyn before heading toward the front staircase.

With every movement, the wooden steps creaked under their feet. When they reached the top, the last stair popped and cracked.

"I can't believe the steps still make noises. It used to annoy my mother, but my father refused to fix the problem."

Outside of the first room, Logan turned to Caitlyn. "Why didn't your dad have them repaired?"

Caitlyn wrapped her arms around her waist. "He said it would come in handy when I became a teenager and tried to stay out past my curfew."

Logan half smiled, believing the steps may have stirred up painful memories from Caitlyn's past. He couldn't imagine how difficult it must have been for her to lose both parents at such a young age. “The noise might have come from this room.” He reached for the doorknob and turned.

“That’s the main bedroom. I’m hoping it’s in decent enough shape for Henry and me to sleep in while we’re here.”

Henry’s eyes widened. “I’m not sleeping in a room with a bear.”

Logan laughed. “I promise there are no bears in this house.”

They moved inside the bedroom. Logan spotted the source of the sound. “I think the barnyard cat decided he wanted to upgrade.” The animal sprinted across the room and into the bathroom.

“Cool! I always wanted a cat. Can we keep him, Mom?”

“I thought you wanted a snake?” Logan glanced at Caitlyn.

Henry shrugged his shoulders. “I don’t care which one. Mom has never let me have a pet.”

Dogs had always been a constant throughout Logan’s childhood. Now, as an adult, he trained service dogs. “Well, cats are pretty low maintenance, so maybe she’ll change her mind.”

“I doubt a stray cat would enjoy the car ride back to Wyoming. He belongs here.” Caitlyn paused. “Well, not here exactly. We’ll have to take him outside and figure out how he got in.”

Logan moved inside the bathroom. “I don’t think you’ll have to worry about the cat. It appears he found the escape route.” He pointed to the window, open enough for the animal to come and go. With some force, Logan pushed the window closed and attempted to secure the lock. “It’s broken. I’ll have to change the lock.”

If Caitlyn planned to sleep in the house, he’d have to do

a thorough search of the property. But, even then, it wasn't a good idea for them to stay here alone. Hopefully, he could convince her to settle at his brother's place. Luke and his family lived in Whispering Slopes, Virginia, so his house in Bluebell sat vacant most of the time.

Twenty minutes later, Logan had taken Caitlyn and Henry on a tour through the entire house. Henry went outside in search of the stray cat while Caitlyn ran out to her car. She returned with a red journal and pen in hand. While moving around the kitchen, she began furiously scribbling page after page of notes.

"Are you making a to-do list?" Logan broke the silence, filling the room.

Caitlyn dropped her hands to her sides but continued to clutch the journal and pen. "It's becoming more like a book than a list." She blew a stray piece of hair away from her face. "I'm pretty good with do-it yourself projects, but I don't think I'll be able to put the house on the market as soon as I had hoped."

Logan couldn't help but wonder if someone special was waiting for her back in Wyoming, but he didn't want to pry. "What's the big rush?" Or did he? "Don't you want to spend time with your son in the town where you grew up?"

"Wyoming is our home."

He was still unsure of her reason for rushing, but it seemed best not to pressure Caitlyn. It appeared she had things on her mind that she'd rather keep private. He could respect that. Logan was a private man himself. "You could always cut the price and sell the house as is. The repairs on the first floor alone could take weeks."

"Time is something I don't have," Caitlyn snapped. "I'm sorry. I didn't mean to be rude."

Logan considered Caitlyn's response. Something wasn't right. Was she in some sort of trouble?

Caitlyn moved to the window over the kitchen sink and whirled around. "Cutting the price isn't an option. Many of the repairs I can do on my own, but I'll need to hire an electrician and plumber."

"I can recommend a few."

"I'd appreciate it." She took a peek inside the journal then closed it shut. "Martha left around fifteen hundred dollars in her will for home repairs."

Logan didn't want to alarm Caitlyn, but given the problems they'd uncovered during their tour, the repairs would eat up the allocated funds in no time. Money could be an issue, or lack of, in Caitlyn's case. He couldn't let his brother's friend make the repairs herself. "I can help you with most of the projects."

"That won't be necessary."

Caitlyn repositioned her stance. It wasn't Logan's imagination. She'd planted her feet against the floor, ready for a fight. Luke had always said Caitlyn was stubborn. His brother hadn't been joking. The woman didn't want his help, but she was kidding herself if she believed she could do everything on her own.

A crack of thunder sounded outside.

"We better get Henry inside. These storms can pack a punch." Logan headed to the front door. Caitlyn tossed the journal as they moved past the dining room table.

"Wow! It's pouring!" Henry flew in through the door the moment Logan pulled it open.

"You're soaked," Caitlyn said.

"I saw some towels in the upstairs hall closet. I'll run and grab some," Logan offered, running to the stairs, taking them two at a time.

Once at the top of the steps, the overhead lights flickered at the same time thunder rattled the walls. The surrounding space went dark. Rain pounded against the roof. A window at the end of the hall provided no outside light. No surprise there. From what Logan had seen during their walk-through of the farmhouse, every window needed a thorough cleaning.

He opened the closet door. A musty aroma shot up his nose. Logan fumbled in the dark space and snatched two bath towels before heading downstairs.

The entire first level of the house was as dark as the upper floor. "Here you go." Logan handed off the towels to Caitlyn. "I better look around for some candles. There's no telling how long we'll be without power, so we don't want to only rely on our phone flashlight."

Inside the kitchen, Logan checked each drawer. Martha appeared to be a packrat. Every drawer was overflowing with odds and ends. Who needed four pairs of scissors? He threw them back and continued to work his way around the room.

"Have you found any candles? It's getting darker outside." Caitlyn entered the room with Henry at her side, swaddled in a towel.

"Not even a flashlight. But if you need any scissors, there's no shortage of those."

Caitlyn moved into the dining room and opened a drawer in the breakfront. "Here they are." She pulled out a handful of tapered candles in a variety of colors.

"How did you know to look there?"

"Some people use their dining room table a couple times of the year for holidays or family gatherings. Usually, they'll light candles for the occasion." Caitlyn stuck one candle in each holder on the tabletop. "Now, if we can find some matches, we'll be good to go."

"I saw one of those long plastic lighters in the drawer beside the stove." Logan scurried to the kitchen and grabbed the lighter. Seconds later, the candles' warm glow softened the room.

"That's much better." Caitlyn pulled out a chair at the table and took a seat. She snatched the journal and scribbled inside.

"You must go through a lot of those," Logan laughed.

Caitlyn's face flushed. "I'm a little obsessed with notebooks and journals, so I stay well-stocked."

"Mom plans everything," Henry shared.

"Well, I hope you leave a little time for unexpected events. Sometimes they make the greatest memories." Following the sudden loss of his fiancée, Logan had quickly learned that every day was a gift that no one should take for granted.

"I'll keep that in mind." Caitlyn wiped her cheek and shook her head. "Something dripped on me?"

Logan looked up and spotted a large water stain on the ceiling. "That's coming from the guest bathroom."

"You didn't leave the water running when you used the restroom, did you?" Caitlyn asked Henry.

"I don't think so." Henry took off up the stairs.

"Wait, you need some light." Logan slipped his cell phone from his back pocket. He turned on the flashlight and chased after the child. Caitlyn followed, clutching her journal.

Inside the bathroom, water spilled over the top of the toilet, covering the floor.

"I didn't mean to break it." Henry blew out a sigh.

Logan squatted and reached for the valve to shut off

the water flow. "It's not your fault. The pipes in this house are old."

Once again, Caitlyn put pen to paper, scribbling in her notebook. "Do you think every pipe will need to be replaced?" Her eyes darted around the room before focusing in Logan's direction.

Logan stood and dusted off his jeans. "Of course, an inspection needs to be done, but my guess is yes. If you want to sell the property for a good price, new piping would be a wise investment."

Henry moved to Logan's side. "My mom doesn't have any money."

"Henry!" Caitlyn slammed the journal shut. "Please, if it's okay, take Mr. Logan's phone and go back down to the kitchen and wait for me."

Logan nodded and passed the device.

Henry obeyed his mother's command and scurried down the steps.

Years ago, Logan had his own financial struggles. Keeping them private was understandable. "My offer still stands. I'm sure you can handle some repairs on your own, but getting this place ready to list on the market is going to be a huge undertaking. There's no way one person could do everything, especially if time is an issue. Please, let me help you."

Caitlyn took a shuddery breath. "But I can't pay you."

Without a mortgage on the property, the proceeds from the sale could pay for the repairs and more, unless Caitlyn was flat broke and carrying debt. Her reaction to Henry's comment caused Logan to believe that could be the case. An idea percolated in his mind. But would she go for it? He wasn't so sure. Something told Logan that Caitlyn might have more than financial struggles hidden in her closet.

Chapter Two

Money. Even when Caitlyn had it, she'd didn't care to discuss it, especially with a total stranger. She inhaled sharply. But Logan wasn't a *complete* stranger. Still, she had no intention of building any relationships during her time in Bluebell. That rule applied to the hunky older brother of a dear friend whom the younger Caitlyn had fallen head over heels for the first time she'd laid eyes on him.

An hour later, the storm had passed and the gusty winds were now nothing but a midafternoon gentle spring breeze. A cardinal chirped outside on a nearby branch. With the electricity restored, pen poised over the open journal, Caitlyn made some quick calculations at the dining room table. Henry and Logan were outside cleaning up tree limbs on the driveway and in the front yard.

Her mind drifted to what Logan had said. Who was she kidding? He was right. She'd never be able to complete the repairs on her own. The material alone would eat up every dollar Martha had left in her will. With a firm grip on the pen, she scratched through the numbers on the page. Tears threatened, but she swallowed hard to tamp them down. A couple of hours earlier, she had believed the house was the answer to her prayers, but the fact remained it was doing nothing but adding to her debt.

"Mom! Come quick!"

Outside, Henry's cry for help sent Caitlyn's protective-momma-bear's instincts into overdrive. She pushed herself away from the table. The chair legs screeched across the wooden floor. She slammed the journal closed and raced outside.

The dilapidated screen door closed with a bang behind Caitlyn. From the porch, she scanned the property and spotted Henry and Logan across the pasture. She bolted down the steps and across the muddy grass. Pumping her arms, her favorite leather boots sunk into the ground, kicking up clods of mud against the back of her pink button-up blouse.

"Look! The fence is totally smashed." Henry pointed to a portion of the split-rail fencing surrounding the property.

Caitlyn skidded to a stop and attempted to catch her breath. "You scared me," she sputtered. "I thought you got hurt."

Logan rested his hand on her arm. "He's fine. He got a little excited by the fallen tree, that's all."

"Sorry. I didn't mean to scare you, but look! The tree is gigantic!"

Neon dollar signs flashed in Caitlyn's mind. To remove a tree that size would be another major expense. She'd used a chain saw a few times, but with other projects on her ever-growing list, it would take her until next spring to get the house ready to sell. She inhaled a calming breath. "Yes, but I'll get it taken care of. I'm sure there are plenty of tree services in the area." She turned to Logan for confirmation.

"Of course, there are. But why would you want to hire someone when there are plenty of able-bodied men ready and willing to do the work for free?"

Confused, Caitlyn tossed Logan a questioning look.

"My brothers and I can get it out of here in no time."

Logan slipped his hands into the back pockets of his jeans as he assessed the damage. "Besides, this would make great firewood. The temperature here drops pretty low in the winter months."

"I appreciate the offer, but I wouldn't think of imposing on you or your brothers."

Logan crossed his arms over his chest. "Since you used to live here, you probably remember what it's like in Bluebell. We help others in their time of need. That's what being a tight-knit community is about. We don't pay to have work done when we can do it ourselves with the help of a neighbor or two."

Caitlyn had no intention of becoming part of this community for a second time, so accepting the help from the residents wouldn't be right. "That's great for you, but I don't live here anymore. And I don't plan on ever making this my home again, so accepting help isn't an option."

Logan laughed. "Boy, my brother Luke was right."

"About what?" Caitlyn questioned.

"You are stubborn."

"No, I'm being realistic. I won't be around to return the favor," Caitlyn stated.

"Fair enough, but what if we made a deal?" Logan's left brow arched.

Dealmaking wasn't Caitlyn's style, but neither was carrying a heap of debt. Prior to Henry's medical issues, she'd never owed a dime to anyone. She'd even had the suggested six-month reserves saved in her bank account. That was long gone now. "I'm not sure. What did you have in mind?"

Logan cleared his throat. "For a couple of years, my livestock have grazed on the land I've been leasing from Martha. However, I have a new idea for the property that I'm currently working on. I had planned on making an offer to purchase the acreage, but she never returned my phone calls. I assumed since she didn't respond to my voice mails, she wasn't interested in selling."

Caitlyn wasn't sure what this had to do with her dire situation. She continued to listen while keeping a close eye on Henry as he skipped rocks in the creek that meandered through the property.

"Since the land is yours now, I thought I could make you an offer."

Hope bubbled. "You want to buy the land? What about the house?" If Logan purchased the property along with the farmhouse, perhaps she and Henry could head back to Wyoming sooner than expected.

Logan shook his head. "I don't have a need for another residence. The couple of hundred acres I've been leasing is all I'm interested in owning."

Caitlyn's heart sunk. Her chance for a quick exit out of town slipped away. "I don't plan on splitting up the property. I'm sure I could command a larger price by selling the house and the land together."

"That's true. But think about the money you'll save on repairs."

"I'm not sure I'm following you."

"You didn't let me finish," Logan continued. "If you allow me to purchase the land I've been leasing, I'll help you get the house and the remaining property ready to sell. You'll have little out-of-pocket expenses."

"With so many repairs needed, I can't take your time. It's as valuable as my own." Caitlyn's suspicions rose. Logan was Luke's brother and she could always trust Luke, yet something didn't sit right with her. Who works for free?

"I'm a rancher, so I'm not on anyone's clock. My brothers and I also train service dogs. I choose how I want to spend my time. The land is important for the growth of my business. If a new owner takes over, he or she might not allow me to continue with the lease, much less buy the property. That's a risk I can't take."

Caitlyn considered Logan's argument.

"Plus, you're my brother's friend. Luke would never let me live it down if I didn't come to the aid of his old friend. You'll be helping me as much as I'm helping you. I can't afford to lose the land."

"Your time may be free, but what about the electrical work and the plumbing? You said yourself a professional would be required for those jobs. I can't let you cover those expenses."

Logan nodded. "As I mentioned, this town is full of people who live to help their neighbor. We have retired folks with great trade skills. Many worked as plumbers and electricians. They love to keep their hands and minds sharp by helping others."

"Thanks, but I don't accept charity. I won't have strangers working for free."

Caitlyn couldn't wrap her head around the idea of people working for no pay. Lately, she hadn't had time to make friends within her community. She worked long hours to keep up with Henry's medical bills. Most of the people she knew were the parents of Henry's classmates, and they were merely acquaintances. Most of the girls enrolled in her barrel racing classes weren't local thanks to some savvy online marketing that had proved beneficial. Many parents drove a couple of hours round-trip for their child's once-a-week class. Apart from her neighbor, Caitlyn didn't have many people she could call if she needed help. But that was okay, at least for this season in her life. She and Henry managed.

"They wouldn't exactly be working for free."

Caitlyn's guilt eased. "I would never expect someone to do that."

"A homemade pie or a plate of cookies is all anyone would accept as payment. Well, maybe old George Dunaway might order up a meat loaf." Logan rubbed his stomach.

Caitlyn laughed and rolled her eyes. "You're kidding, right?"

"I never kid about food. George doesn't either," Logan laughed.

Chewing on her lower lip, Caitlyn's mind raced while she considered her options. But what were they? Earlier, she'd tried to make a list in her notebook, but the page had remained blank because there were no options. Either she made a deal with Logan, or she'd go deeper into debt trying to repair the old house. There wouldn't be any money from the proceeds of the sale to pay the medical bills or her back rent. Her inheritance would end up costing her money. As much as she wanted to handle the situation on her own, she couldn't.

"What do you say?" Logan waited for an answer.

Caitlyn looked up at the house in defeat. She remained silent for a moment before slowly extending her hand. "It's a deal."

Logan gripped the wrench to tighten the doorknob on the kitchen door leading to the back patio. Since getting Caitlyn to agree to his deal, everything he touched in the house seemed to break, fall off, or didn't work at all. Before he could begin making phone calls to recruit help, he'd need to make a master list of things that required immediate attention. Logan laughed to himself. Maybe he should check with Caitlyn. She may have already created that list.

The front screen door slammed.

"What should I do with the suitcase, Mom?"

"You can put it in the main bedroom."

Logan leaned toward the voices and shook his head. When Caitlyn mentioned staying in the house, he'd thought she'd been joking. He'd been wrong. Logan slid the wrench into his back pocket, readying himself for a disagreement once he reminded Caitlyn the house was in no condition for overnight guests.

Logan stepped into the dining room and found Caitlyn. Once again, she sat hunched at the table, writing in her notebook.

Henry stepped onto the stair landing.

"Hold up, buddy."

Henry stopped and put the suitcase down.

Logan approached the table. "Why don't I drive you into town so you can get checked into the hotel? Kathleen Kilby owns the Sleep Inn. She'll take good care of you and Henry."

Caitlyn lifted her head and held a strong posture. "We plan to stay here."

Exactly the response he'd expected. "I don't think it's a good idea. You'd both be more comfortable and safer staying in town."

"All we need is a bed to rest our heads. Besides, I can easily replace the lock on the main bathroom window."

"What about meals?" He clasped his hands behind his back. "We haven't checked the stove. I doubt anyone has used it since Martha left town."

"The refrigerator seems to work fine. I'm sure the stove is okay, too. We aren't going to a hotel, so let's drop the subject."

It appeared hopeless. No matter what he said, Logan

would not change Caitlyn's mind. But he had to try. "Okay, no hotel. How about you stay at Luke's place? His primary residence is in Virginia, but he has a place here. If I called him now, I'm sure he'd offer it to you."

"That won't be necessary." Caitlyn turned to Henry. "Take the suitcase upstairs."

Henry took off before Logan could say anything more. It was just as well. He'd be wasting his breath. Caitlyn was adamant. "At least let me drive you into town to pick up some sheets for the bed and some groceries."

Caitlyn smiled. "I'd appreciate that, but I thought maybe Henry and I could drive to Denver to get what we need."

Logan glanced at his watch. "It's getting a little late to make that drive. By the time you made it home, it would be dark."

"That's what headlights are for," Caitlyn laughed.

He liked her quick wit. "I suppose you're right, but there are tons of critters on the roads at night. I wouldn't be comfortable with you and Henry traveling alone." It wasn't the wildlife Logan worried about. The city was full of dangerous people. Something he'd never thought much about until his fiancée hadn't returned from her trip.

"Okay, you win." Caitlyn held up her hands. "The last thing I need is a car repair bill on top of everything else. Let me run upstairs and get Henry. I want to change into something a little more presentable, if you don't mind."

"Of course, but I think you look great the way you are." Logan noticed Caitlyn's cheeks redden. "I'm sorry. I didn't mean to sound forward. It's just—we're pretty casual around here."

"I'll keep that in mind." She turned and headed up the stairs.

Logan watched until she rounded the corner. The woman would look great dressed in a potato sack.

A few minutes later, Logan opened the passenger door of his truck for Caitlyn. She climbed aboard wearing a pair of khaki pants and a yellow blouse. A shiny gloss highlighted her naturally pink lips.

"I'll get Henry fastened in the back seat," Logan offered. "Don't worry. I have booster seats for my niece and nephew."

"I can do it myself." Henry jumped once and then again.

"It's a little too high for you, buddy. Let me help you." Logan hoisted Henry into the truck and buckled him in.

"Do you remember Garrison's Mercantile Company?" Logan asked, turning on the main road into town.

"It's still open?"

Logan nodded. "It sure is. The place is a historical landmark. Hank and Nellie are both pushing eighty, but they're still going strong. They plan to pass the store on to their son if they ever decide to retire."

"I remember my mother taking me every Saturday for an ice cream cone before we'd shop for groceries," Caitlyn remarked, gazing out the window.

Logan hoped he'd sparked a fond memory for Caitlyn.

"One time, Mr. Garrison gave me two extra scoops after my mother told him the next day was my birthday. My small hands could hardly hold on to the cone. One scoop rolled off the top and hit the floor. When I started crying, Mr. Garrison ran to me carrying a bowl with four scoops."

"That's Hank all right." Logan was relieved the memory was a good one.

"Do you think he'll give me some ice cream?" Henry called out from the back seat.

Logan chuckled. "I'm sure he will."

Caitlyn slipped the ubiquitous journal from her bag and began writing. "I'll make a grocery list."

"Make sure you include a couple of flashlights and batteries. We could have more storms, like earlier today," Logan said.

"I sure hope not. The last thing I need is for another falling tree to damage the fencing."

"Try not to worry so much. Cleaning up the tree and repairing the fence won't be a big deal." Logan hit the turn signal and pulled into Garrison's gravel parking lot. "We're here."

"The place hasn't changed a bit." Caitlyn unfastened her seat belt and exited the vehicle.

Logan stepped out of the truck, helped Henry from the back seat, and they headed inside.

The bell over the front door jangled, and the aroma of freshly baked cookies filled the store.

"Nellie must be baking this afternoon." Logan inhaled the sweet scent.

"Oh, my goodness." The petite, gray-haired woman scurried from behind the counter with open arms. "Caitlyn Calloway, I knew you'd come home one day."

"Hello, Mrs. Garrison." Caitlyn closed the distance and wiped a tear.

Logan watched while the women held each other.

"You're grown up now. Please call me Nellie." The woman pulled away, her eyes damp with tears. "You look just like your mother." Nellie moved her gaze to Henry. "And who do we have here?"

Henry grinned and stepped forward. "I'm Henry. Did you know my mom when she lived here?"

"I did." Nellie reached out her hand. "It's nice to meet you, Henry. I've got cookies fresh from the oven." She turned to the counter and picked up a yellow plate. "They're still warm." She held the cookies in front of Henry.

The boy's eyes widened and he helped himself. "Chocolate chip are my favorite." Henry took a big bite and reached for a second.

"Caitlyn and Henry plan to stay at Martha's place for a while. We need to pick up some groceries and other supplies." Logan looked around. "Is Hank here or at the house?"

"He's in the office on the phone." Nellie quickly turned to Caitlyn. "From what I hear, the farm is yours now. I think it's wonderful that Martha left the house and land to you. That's where you belong."

"My mom wants to sell it, but I think it would be cool to live here."

"Sell? But it's your home, dear." Nellie flashed a look of concern.

Caitlyn shifted her weight. "Our home is in Wyoming now. I came back to sell the property. Unfortunately, it needs a lot of work before it's ready to go on the market."

Logan knew Nellie would do everything in her power to convince Caitlyn to stay, but from what he could tell, that was going to be a losing battle. "That's what I wanted to speak with Hank about. I had hoped he could round up some of his ranch hands to help with the repairs."

"I'm sure they'd be happy to lend a hand. Nelson Whitfield was here last week to replace our hot water tank. Let me run back and see if Hank's off the phone."

Nellie shuffled toward the office but stopped short and turned. "Henry, you help yourself to more of those cookies on the counter."

"Thanks!" The boy ran to the plate.

Logan followed and snatched one. "You better grab one

for yourself before Henry devours them," he said to Caitlyn, who had her face buried in her journal.

She looked up. "Is Nelson a plumber?"

Logan nodded. "Yes, but he's also a wiz with appliance repairs. He retired about ten years ago, but he keeps busy helping others around town with their plumbing issues. So you can check 'find plumber' off of your list." He winked.

"Mom, don't forget to get some cereal for my breakfast."

"I've got it on my list. Pick out an inexpensive box with little sugar." Caitlyn marked her sheet.

"Hold up, Henry. I know chocolate-chip cookies are your favorite, but have you tried chocolate-chip pancakes?" Logan asked.

"I've never had that. Mom always makes blueberry pancakes. They're okay." Henry shrugged his shoulders.

"I make pancakes on Saturday mornings. Growing up, it's something my mother did for me and my brothers, so I've held on to the tradition." Logan glanced in Caitlyn's direction and she smiled. "If it's okay with your mom, maybe I can come over tomorrow morning and make you chocolate-chip pancakes." Logan had concerns about the safety of the stove and other appliances in the house. This would give him the opportunity to check them out. "I have the ingredients, so you won't need to purchase anything."

Henry bounced on his toes. "That sounds awesome! It's okay, right, Mom?" Henry waited for a response.

Caitlyn twisted a strand of her hair and watched her son's excitement. "Well, we don't want to inconvenience you, but the pancakes do sound delicious."

Logan had expected Caitlyn to decline the offer, but perhaps she didn't want to disappoint Henry. What if she'd said no? Logan wondered if he would have been more disappointed than Henry.

Chapter Three

Why had she agreed to Saturday-morning pancakes with Logan? Caitlyn stood in front of the bathroom mirror and secured the loose bun with a claw clip. She had agreed, for Henry's sake. Everything she did was for her son. But, she had to admit, she was excited to see Logan for breakfast as well.

Caitlyn glanced at her reflection and blew out an exasperated breath. Concealer. The dark circles beneath her eyes were proof of a restless night. Caitlyn wasn't frightened to sleep in her childhood home, but the squeaks and creaks throughout the night had kept her tossing and turning. The sagging-middle mattress hadn't helped either. Of course, Henry was out the moment his head hit the pillow.

Caitlyn fumbled through her cosmetic bag and eyed her watch. Logan would be here in ten minutes, and she still resembled a raccoon.

"Mom, there's water on the floor," Henry called out from downstairs.

Caitlyn dabbed two dots of makeup under each eye and blended it into her skin. "I'll be down in a second." She zipped the bag closed, grabbed her journal off the vanity, and headed downstairs to investigate.

The hardwood at the bottom of the staircase was dry. With

a quick scan of her surroundings, she spotted wet shoe prints outside of the doorway to the kitchen. She moved closer and found Henry stomping his new tennis shoes in the puddles of water that covered the floor. "Henry! You're making a mess."

"It's not me. It's that white thing." Henry pointed to the mudroom off the kitchen.

"That's the hot water heater." That would explain the cold shower she'd endured this morning and probably the hissing and knocking she'd heard last night.

"Don't worry, Mom. Mr. Logan can have that guy Nelson come and fix it."

Caitlyn relaxed her shoulders. Sometimes Henry knew exactly the right thing to say to calm her nerves. "You're right. Thank you for reminding me."

A knock at the front door sounded. Caitlyn had her hands on the mop inside the pantry. "That must be Mr. Logan. Can you go let him in?"

"Sure!" Henry shot out of the room, leaving behind a path of shoe prints through the kitchen.

Within seconds, Logan ran into the kitchen and stopped short of the water covering the floor.

"The water heater is leaking," Caitlyn shouted from the pantry.

"Have you turned off the shutoff valve?"

"No, I was upstairs when Henry yelled." Caitlyn glanced over her shoulder before continuing with the mop.

"Don't panic. I'll take care of it." Logan moved into the mudroom.

Forty-five minutes later, Nelson had come by to assess the problem with the water tank. He replaced a corroded valve, but recommended replacing the tank to prevent further issues.

Settled at the kitchen table, Caitlyn clenched her teeth

in frustration as she reviewed her list of repairs. On a positive note, with Nelson's help, Logan had completed the inspection of the stove and everything seemed to be in working order.

"Grab a plate, Henry." Logan stood at the stove with his broad back to her. He flipped the pancake and called over his shoulder.

The sweet aroma of the milk chocolate chips melting inside the skillet calmed Caitlyn's nerves. "Those smell delicious."

Logan piled two more cakes on Henry's stack. "Okay, let me get some ready for your mom." He passed the plate to Henry before turning to pour three circles of batter. The oversize skillet sizzled. "Yours will be ready in a couple of minutes." He tossed a grin at Caitlyn before wiping up a dollop of batter he'd dripped on the counter.

Caitlyn admired Logan's cooking skills. He followed the clean-as-you-go method to avoid dealing with a big mess after the meal, something she remembered her mother had done.

"Oh man! These are so good." Henry shoveled another bite into his mouth. "Can I come over to your house next Saturday?"

The last thing Caitlyn wanted was for Henry to break her own rule to not get attached to anyone or anything in Bluebell. It would make it that much harder on him once she sold the house and they headed back to Wyoming. Caitlyn picked up the napkin and wiped the melted chocolate from Henry's chin. "Sweetie, it's not polite to invite yourself to someone's house."

Logan ferried Caitlyn's serving and placed it on the table. He ruffled the top of Henry's hair. "You're welcome to come over anytime. Sometimes it gets a little quiet for me and Rocky."

"Who's Rocky?" Henry asked.

"He's my German shepherd." Logan settled into the empty chair across from Henry with a cup of coffee.

Henry's eyes widened. "Wow! I've seen those dogs before. He must be huge."

Logan beamed. "He's seventy-five pounds."

Caitlyn nudged Henry's shoulder. "Rocky weighs more than you do," she laughed.

"Maybe I can meet him tomorrow." Henry sat up straighter in his chair.

"Henry! What did I say about inviting yourself to Mr. Logan's house?" Caitlyn shook her head and looked at Logan. "I'm sorry."

Logan smiled at Henry. "I'll be at church in the morning, but you and your mom are welcome to come over in the afternoon for lunch. Rocky is only a year old, and he's still growing. He's got a lot of energy and loves to meet new people."

"Can we go, Mom? Please." Henry pouted adorably.

Against her better judgment, Caitlyn nodded. "Okay."

"Great, you can meet Rocky and Sophie."

Caitlyn's ears perked up. Sophie? Logan didn't wear a wedding ring. Perhaps Sophie was his girlfriend.

"Who's Sophie?" Henry asked, finishing the last bite of his breakfast.

Caitlyn opened her mouth but quickly pressed her lips together. It was natural for kids to be inquisitive. At least, that's what she told herself. Besides, she couldn't deny she was a little curious about Sophie, too, so she held her peace.

"Sophie is a rescue dog I'm training. She's a Labrador retriever."

"Cool. What are you training it to do?" Henry eagerly waited for Logan's answer.

"She's being trained to become a service dog."

Intrigued, Caitlyn settled back against her chair. "You mentioned you and your brother's train service dogs. We'd love to hear more about it. Right, Henry?" She glanced at her son.

Henry quickly nodded and leaned in, placing his elbows on the table.

"My brothers and I started Beckett's Canine Training. Our goal is to improve the quality of life for individuals with disabilities and other physical impairments. We specifically train each dog to meet the exact needs of its master," Logan explained.

"So what will Sophie do?"

Logan glanced at Caitlyn before answering Henry's question. "Sophie is being trained to be a seeing-eye dog."

"What's that?" Henry's face scrunched.

"They are service dogs trained to help people who can't see. The animal becomes their owner's eyes and helps them to navigate a world of darkness. They help to keep them safe."

Henry's eyes popped. "Wow! That's what you do?" Henry placed his hand over his eyes. "Not seeing anything must be hard. I'd be running into everything."

Logan nodded. "It is difficult. Our eyes are one of the many blessings God has provided, unfortunately not everyone can see, so we train the dogs to take over."

Caitlyn's heart warmed at Logan's sweet explanation. From what she'd seen so far in his interactions with Henry, Logan was great with children. Of course, that's what she'd believed about her ex-boyfriend. She'd trusted him and, as their relationship had grown, she'd allowed the man to be a part of Henry's life. That had proved to be a grave mistake; one that had caused her to question her judgment in men. Caitlyn wouldn't allow her painful history to repeat itself. Protecting Henry was her job. Allowing him to form an attachment to Logan was a risk she couldn't take. Maybe accepting Logan's lunch invitation hadn't been such a good idea.

Sunday morning, following a period of fellowship in the hall, Logan stepped outside the church and breathed in the fresh, sun-drenched air. He moved across the gravel parking area with an extra spring in his step. Sure, the sermon this morning had been uplifting, but his heightened mood was present the moment he'd planted his feet on the floor upon waking up. Caitlyn and Henry were coming over this afternoon. He couldn't deny the excitement he felt about their impending visit.

Last night, a few buddies had invited him to a baseball game in Denver. Logan had declined the invitation and stayed home to prepare for his lunch guests. He'd used his mother's family recipe to make extra-crispy fried chicken and cheesy scalloped potatoes. For dessert, Logan planned to serve German chocolate cake from Garrison's market. Since Nellie didn't bake on Sunday, she'd taken his order late yesterday and made the cake last night. Nellie brought the treat to church, saving him a trip into town.

Logan climbed into the truck, placed the cake on the floor of the passenger seat and removed his cell phone from his glove compartment. He'd made a habit of keeping the device outside of church after an embarrassing incident a couple of months ago. During the benediction, his phone, which he'd thought was on vibrate, blasted the sound of various farm animals. Unbeknownst to Logan, his brother Jake had playfully changed his ring tone the day before, never imagining it would go off in the middle of church services.

"Hey, buddy." Nelson approached the open window of Logan's truck.

Logan turned the engine off and exited the vehicle. "Thanks again for taking care of the water heater yesterday. I'm sorry if I interrupted your Saturday."

"The only thing you interrupted was a chance to chip away at Thelma's never-ending honey-do list," Nelson laughed.

Logan's expression wavered as he looked at his friend. He had longed to have such a list. Marriage and family were things he'd always wanted and assumed one day he would have. The years had passed quickly without meeting the right person—until Melody. With her, Logan had found a love to last a lifetime. So why hadn't he protected her? He should have been there in her last moments. It should have been him. *Throw it into the air. Let God deal with the questions of why.* That's what Pastor Kidd had told him to do, but the guilt and regret remained.

"I know Caitlyn was thankful you could make the repair."

"That's what I wanted to talk with you about. Like I mentioned yesterday, the repair was a temporary fix, so it's probably a matter of time before the tank fails. When that happens, it could create substantial water damage." Nelson frowned.

Logan nodded, and a muscle in his jaw knotted. "I think Caitlyn is hoping to sell the house before that happens. With the cosmetic repairs alone, she's overwhelmed by the potential costs involved." The constant scribbling in her journal was proof the house was causing anxiety.

Nelson reached inside the jacket of his Sunday suit and pulled out a package of chewing gum. He held it out to Logan.

"Thanks." Logan removed the foil and popped the piece into his mouth.

Nelson did the same before tucking the pack away. "I have some news that might ease Caitlyn's worries a bit. I got a text last night from a buddy over in Mineral Springs. He's always buying the latest and great appliance. A couple of days ago, he bought a tankless water heater."

Logan had considered purchasing one for his house since his tank was up in the attic. If it ever went out, he could imagine the mess it would create. "I hear those are great, but probably out of Caitlyn's budget."

"That's the good news. Jeb offered me his existing heater for free. And the best part is, it's a significant upgrade from what she's got now, since his tank is shy of three years old."

Logan was delighted at the blessing. Caitlyn could check "addressing the water heater" from her list without spending a penny. "That's fantastic news. Caitlyn will be thrilled."

"I told Jeb I'd come by in the morning and install his new unit, so I'll have Caitlyn's on my truck whenever she's ready."

"That sounds good. She's coming by for lunch this afternoon, so I'll let her know."

Nelson grinned. "Oh, really?"

Logan knew Nelson's mind was churning with possibilities. He and his wife were the ones who'd introduced Logan and Melody. Three years earlier, the matchmaking couple had invited them to Sunday dinner. Thelma had known Melody since she was a child, and believed she was perfect for Logan. Thelma had been right. After that dinner, Logan and Melody had practically been inseparable.

Logan held up his hand. "Hold on. I see you're going into matchmaking mode. It's not what you think. The main reason I invited Caitlyn over was for Henry to meet Rocky and Sophie. The boy was curious yesterday when I mentioned I'm training Sophie. I thought it might be good for him to see firsthand how a seeing-eye dog can change a person's life for the better."

"Okay, whatever you say." Nelson chuckled. "When Caitlyn brings Henry over to meet the dogs—" Nelson threw in a wink "—you can ask her when it's convenient for me to install her new water heater."

There was no changing his mind about a love connection. When an idea planted into Nelson Whitfield's head, it took root. "I'll do that." Logan extended his hand in gratitude. "Thanks again for everything. And please, tell Jeb I said thank you as well."

Nelson nodded and turned on his heel.

For the second time since church had ended, Logan climbed back into his truck. More excited than he'd been when he'd first woken up this morning, he glanced at the time on his dashboard. Caitlyn and Henry weren't due to arrive at his house for three hours. No doubt she was home worrying and adding items to her to-do list. Energized by Nelson's surprise, Logan couldn't wait to share the good news with Caitlyn and hopefully calm her nerves. He'd pop by her house on his way home.

Ten minutes into the drive, Logan had the windows down and his favorite country station playing. Before church, he'd met up with a few fellas who'd offered to help with the exterior repairs. Since the extended weather forecast showed no chance of rain, tomorrow was a good day to start the work. Everything was falling into place. Caitlyn would be pleased.

Logan turned the wheel of his truck onto the gravel driveway. He spotted Caitlyn's SUV in front of the house. A faint aroma of smoke filled the cab of his vehicle as he unfastened his seat belt. Once outside, his eyes popped when he spotted flames shooting from the roof of the old farmhouse. He sprinted toward the front door, knowing Caitlyn and Henry were inside.

Chapter Four

Caitlyn stood in the front yard after the Bluebell Canyon Volunteer Fire Department extinguished the flames. As she assessed the damage to the home, questions swirled in her head. Should she abandon her plan to make improvements and instead sell the house in its current state? Was the fire an ominous sign to reconsider her idea of using the money from the sale of the property to pay her debt?

"Thanks for saving us, Mr. Logan!" Henry fixed his eyes on Logan.

Earlier, while in the kitchen with Henry, she'd heard Logan pounding on the front door and yelling for them to get out of the house. Caitlyn didn't have a clue what was happening up in the attic. "Yes, thank you, Logan."

"I know what I want to be when I grow up." Henry tugged on his mother's arm.

Caitlyn's eyes were gritty with fatigue, but she managed to raise a curious eyebrow. "What's that?"

"A firefighter. Mr. Jack told me they really need more people. Maybe if we stayed here, I could work for them. Do you think I could?" Henry looked up at Logan.

"Sure, but you need to wait until you're eighteen. Keep in mind, everyone who showed up today is a volunteer."

"What's that mean?"

"They don't get paid. Some leave their full-time jobs in town when there's a fire, while others are retired."

Henry's eyes widened. "Wow! They do all of that work for free?"

Caitlyn admired the commitment the volunteers had for their community. She also had a great respect for the business owners who allowed their employees to leave their job whenever called to assist. It takes an exceptional person to make such a commitment. From what she'd seen so far, this town was full of special people ready and willing to help others. The number of townspeople who'd come to her aid today was overwhelming. They weren't even part of the fire department.

"They love their community and the people. Most have lived here their entire lives, along with past generations," Logan explained.

"That's pretty cool. Mom's my only family. Before her, I moved around a lot," Henry said before he dashed toward a group of volunteers talking on the front porch.

"I adopted Henry two years ago, after being his foster parent for a year. He lived the first four years of his life shuffled from one foster home to the next," Caitlyn told him.

Logan shifted his weight. "I didn't want to pry into your business. My brother never mentioned you'd gotten married, so I kind of wondered about Henry. But like I said, it's not my business." Logan glanced up at the front porch before turning his attention back to Caitlyn. "You're doing a wonderful thing—Henry is a terrific kid. Few people would make the sacrifices you've made."

"Henry had a rough start in life. I wanted him to feel safe. That's why it's important for me to sell this property and get him back to Wyoming as soon as possible. I want him to have stability in his life." Caitlyn couldn't let her son down. Yes, the house she rented in Wyoming was old and had a tiny yard, but it was the only true home Henry had ever known.

"Fortunately, there was only fire damage inside the attic. It could have been a lot worse if it had spread downstairs," Logan noted.

Caitlyn shuddered at the thought. "That's a relief. So what's next? Is it safe for me to go up there and clean?"

"Absolutely not. You need to leave that to the professionals."

Another expense. Caitlyn wasn't seeing a light at the end of this costly tunnel.

"Don't worry. Lester has a buddy in the fire restoration business. He'll come out to remove the smoke and ash properly. Prolonged debris presence amplifies the damage potential because of the acidic nature of the ash. We don't want the smoke to stain the walls."

A chill traveled down Caitlyn's spine. What if the fire had started at night while she and Henry had been sleeping? With so many repairs necessary, she'd neglected to consider whether the smoke detectors worked properly. "If you hadn't shown up, I'm not sure what would have happened."

"It's best if you don't let your mind imagine the worst. According to Lester, faulty wiring caused the fire. He's an electrician by trade, so he can fix the issue that started the fire. He'll also do a complete inspection of the entire house."

Caitlyn crossed her arms. "Yes, definitely. I can't sell the property if there's any risk of this happening again. Have Lester do whatever needs to be done. When it comes to safety, I won't cut corners."

"You can trust Lester." Logan turned his focus upward and pointed. "As for the hole in the roof, I'll take care of that."

"Was the hole caused by the fire?"

Logan shook his head. "No, that was how the squirrel or a chipmunk got into the attic to chew the wiring. Lester has flagged all the wires the critter had sunk its teeth into. He'll be back tomorrow to fix those and to inspect the rest of the house."

After escaping the home and watching flames shoot from the top of the house, Caitlyn realized Logan was right. It wasn't safe for her and Henry to remain in the house. "I suppose Henry and I need to head into town and book a room at the motel for the night." What choice did she have? If it were only her, maybe she'd stay, but she had Henry's safety to consider.

"I hope you don't think I'm out of line, but a motel could end up costing you a lot of money."

Logan's words rang true. It was an added expense she couldn't afford. Addressing the wiring issue would most likely take more than one day. Caitlyn had an emergency credit card with a zero balance tucked away in the side pocket of her wallet. This would definitely fall under the emergency column of her budget.

"Last night, I spoke with Luke. I mentioned you were in town and some issues with the house you've inherited. Before I even asked about you and Henry bunking at his place, he extended the offer." Logan reached out and placed his hand on Caitlyn's arm. "It would make Luke feel good to know he was helping an old friend. Besides, Henry will have a lot more fun exploring Luke's property than hanging out in a motel with a paved parking lot as the front yard."

Caitlyn considered Logan's offer. As much as she wanted to do things on her own, she had to put Henry's safety first.

"Come on. What do you say?" He smiled into her eyes.

She hesitated then smiled back. "Okay. But only until Lester gets the wiring situation repaired."

"Great. I'll shoot a message to Luke and let him know. He'll be thrilled."

"I'd like to send him a thank you text." Caitlyn pulled her phone from the back pocket of her jeans. "I'm sure the number I have for him is outdated."

Caitlyn edited her contact information while Logan recited the numbers. She'd send Luke a message tonight and thank him for his generosity. The years may have passed, but she could tell Luke hadn't changed. A sense of calmness covered her like the first warm blanket of winter. "Thank you. By the way, you know I'm grateful you arrived when you did, but what brought you by? Did you see the smoke from the road?"

"Actually, I didn't see the fire until I arrived at the house. I came by to share some good news with you. Of course, I could have waited until you and Henry came over for lunch, but I suppose I got a little overexcited."

Caitlyn could use some good news. Since her arrival in Bluebell, one expensive problem after another had overwhelmed her. "What's the news?"

"After church service this morning, I ran into Nelson in the parking lot. He's got a practically brand-new water heater whenever you're ready."

This wasn't exactly the good news Caitlyn had hoped to hear, but she didn't want to appear ungrateful. "I appreciate your and Nelson's concern. Since the heater isn't leaking anymore, I should spend my money on repairs that need immediate attention, so I'm able to put the house on the market. Please tell Nelson I said thank you, though."

"I should have made myself clearer. The water heater won't cost you a dime. Nelson's friend purchased an upgraded model, so he has no use for two tanks. Nelson will have it on the back of his truck tomorrow whenever you're ready for him to install it for you." Logan pushed his hands into the front pockets of his jeans.

Caitlyn chewed on her lower lip.

"Look, I know how you feel about accepting charity. But you'd be doing Nelson a favor by getting it off his truck."

Caitlyn listened as Logan explained the history behind the new heater. She glanced over at Henry on the porch, swinging and laughing with Mrs. Garrison. Something he hadn't done a lot of lately. Maybe it was time to check her pride at the door for the well-being of her son and accept the generous offer. Her shoulders relaxed and she took a breath. "I'm sorry if I appeared ungrateful. Replacing the water heater would be one less thing for me to worry about. So yes, tell Nelson he can do the installation whenever he has the time."

Logan sighed silently with relief. "I'll do that—and one more thing."

Caitlyn gave him an assessing look. "What's that?" She couldn't imagine what more good news Logan had for her.

"Don't forget to scratch off replacing the heater from that to-do list of yours," he quipped.

Across the front yard, several men congregated around the cars parked in the driveway. "It looks like the rest of the crew is getting ready to head out. I'm going to go talk with the guys who plan to come by this week to get started on the repairs. Why don't you and Henry pack up your things? You can follow me to Luke's place and we'll get you settled. Then we can head to my house for that lunch I promised. You're probably starving."

Several hours had passed since Caitlyn had cooked waffles for Henry's breakfast. She'd opted for a cup of coffee and a piece of toast. "I am kind of hungry," she conceded.

"Great. We can eat lunch and, after, Henry can meet Rocky and Sophie."

Caitlyn loved dogs. She'd thought about getting a puppy for Henry, but her plans had changed following Henry's diagnosis. Bringing an untrained dog into their home required time and patience—two things she was short on these days. Truthfully, the added expense of welcoming a pet into their home was the main reason she'd frequently had to tell Henry that it wasn't the right time. She glanced up at the farmhouse with the gaping hole in the roof, and her stomach twisted. With so many repairs to be done before she could think about putting the place on the market, Caitlyn wasn't sure how much longer she and Henry would even have a home.

"You probably think I'm just trying to be polite, but honestly, this is the best fried chicken I've ever eaten in my life." Caitlyn sank her teeth into the half-eaten breast, devouring it as if she hadn't had a meal in days.

Logan chuckled and pushed himself away from the solid oak kitchen table. The afternoon sunlight streamed through the oversize windows of his recently renovated farmhouse kitchen. "There's plenty more." He moved to the stainless-steel, six-burner stove and opened the oven door to remove the remaining pieces of chicken.

"I'll have another leg, please," Henry requested.

Logan placed the serving dish on the table. "You got it, buddy." Logan grinned at Henry, and his heart gave a tug.

Henry snatched the piece the second it landed on his plate. His eyes popped when he took a bite. "Why doesn't your chicken taste like this, Mom?"

Caitlyn frowned. "It's healthier when it's baked." She turned her attention back to her meal.

"But not as good. Right, buddy?" Logan winked at Henry.

Henry licked his fingers. "No way."

"Okay, you guys are right," Caitlyn said before reaching for a wing. "Who taught you how to fry chicken like this?"

"It's my mom's recipe. It's been in the family for years. Mom taught all of us Beckett boys to cook. She said it was the best way to win a woman's heart."

Caitlyn wholeheartedly agreed. "I think she might be right."

Logan considered Caitlyn's response while an awkward silence hung in the air. He noted her cheeks turning red.

"I didn't mean… I…um… I mean, it's good for a man to know how to cook."

Logan laughed. He was pretty confident Caitlyn wasn't about to allow any man into her life. He'd sensed her guarded heart since their first meeting. That was one thing they had in common. "I know what you meant. Yeah, my mom was afraid all of her sons would end up starving bachelors."

"Your mom sounds like a smart woman to teach her sons how to be independent. I hope I'm able to do the same with Henry."

Henry jerked his head up. "I don't want to learn to cook. I'll just order takeout like David's dad does."

"Is David a friend from back home?" Logan asked.

"We're not really friends." Henry's smile slipped away. "I don't have a lot of those. He's just a kid in my class. His parents live in different houses now, so his dad orders out when David spends the night."

Henry was a likable kid. Why wouldn't he have friends?

"Knowing how to cook can save you a lot of money. Ordering out can be expensive. Besides, you might enjoy hanging out in the kitchen cooking with your mom. I know I did." Logan would give anything to cook a meal with his mom. Shortly after her Alzheimer's diagnosis, she'd lost the ability to even put together the simplest meal.

Caitlyn dabbed her mouth with the napkin. "Do your parents live in the area?"

Logan felt a stab of sadness. "Actually, my mom is in a memory care facility in Denver."

"I'm sorry to hear that," Caitlyn responded.

"Thanks. My brothers and I helped my dad care for her at home as long as we could. He did an amazing job as her full-time caregiver for several years. As the disease progressed, my dad believed Mom needed specialized medical professionals. That wasn't available here in Bluebell. We're all at peace knowing she's getting the best care. They still have their home here on the family ranch, but my dad stays in a condo in Denver most of the time, so he's able to visit with her every day." Logan admired his father's dedication to his mother. He longed for a relationship like theirs and had thought he'd found it with Melody...until he'd made the worst decision of his life.

Caitlyn looked up at Logan. "Your dad sounds like a wonderful and selfless man."

"I could only hope to be half as good of a man." Logan took a drink of his iced tea.

"When do I get to meet Rocky and Sophie?" Henry downed the last of his drink.

It thrilled Logan to see Henry so excited about the dogs. After hearing his comment about the lack of friends, Sophie and Rocky might be just what he needed. "Well, we can either head outside now or after we've had dessert." Logan glanced in Caitlyn's direction. She was leaning back in her chair with her hands splayed across her stomach.

Caitlyn released a heavy breath. "After all of this delicious food, maybe a nice walk outside would be a good idea. What do you think, Henry?"

"I want to see the dogs!" Henry jumped out of his chair.

"Okay, the German chocolate cake can wait until later." Logan stood up and retrieved the plates from the table. He ferried them across the kitchen and placed them in the sink.

"I can help with those." Caitlyn grabbed the dishtowel from the island and moved toward Logan.

"Thanks, but that's unnecessary. I make a point of not putting my guests to work. I'll take care of this later."

Outside, the brilliant afternoon sun ignited the landscape. Its warmth provided the perfect late springtime temperature.

"Is it always so beautiful this time of year?" Caitlyn gazed up at the cumulus clouds painted across the crystal-blue sky.

"We can have fantastic weather in late May, but it can quickly change. It's good to check your weather app before planning your day."

Caitlyn slid her hands into the back pocket of her jeans. "You're right. I remember as a child wearing a short-sleeved shirt one day and building a snowman the next."

The trio strolled across the grassy field. A gentle breeze moved through the vibrant and colorful wildflowers, creating a soothing rustling sound. A sweet fragrance filled the air.

"Is that water over there?" Henry pointed to the pond on an area of the land Logan currently leased from Martha.

Logan loved the property, particularly the pond. Once he's started leasing the land, it had become his mother's favorite place to sit and spend time with God, which was one of several reasons it was important for him to take ownership of the property. "It sure is. Do you like to fish?"

"I don't know. I've never fished, but I'd sure like to."

Henry bit his lower lip. "My mom doesn't like me to get near water since I don't know how to swim."

Logan's father had taught him and his brothers how to swim almost as soon as they'd learned how to walk. In Whispering Slopes, where he grew up, Logan and his siblings could never wait for that first swim of the season. Against their mother's advice, they'd often jump into the pond on their property in early May. Sometimes the water was so cold he thought his head would freeze. "I don't recall not being able to swim. My father practically threw me and my brothers into the pond and told us to sink or swim."

"Cool! Why can't I do that?" Henry stopped in his tracks and turned to his mother.

"You need to be taught to swim by a professional." Caitlyn rolled her shoulders. "I plan to sign him up for swimming lessons this summer."

Logan nodded. It wasn't his place to interfere, but a boy his age should go fishing. "Maybe if it's okay with your mom, you and I can fish at the pond sometime." Logan eyed Caitlyn with hopes he wasn't overstepping her boundaries. "I'll make sure he doesn't get too close to the water's edge."

Henry ran to his mother's side. "Oh, can I please go fishing with Mr. Logan?"

Caitlyn chewed on her thumbnail, contemplating Henry's request.

"You can come along and supervise. We could have a picnic. Maybe make an afternoon out of it," Logan suggested.

Henry's eyes widened with excitement before he jumped up and down. "Please—can we, Mom? I never get to do anything fun like that at home."

Caitlyn dropped her hands to her sides and looked down at her son. She hesitated before turning to Logan. "That sounds like a wonderful idea and a perfect way to spend an afternoon."

"Awesome!" Henry did a fist pump. He skipped off ahead of the adults.

Out of earshot, Logan stepped closer to Caitlyn. "I didn't mean to overstep my bounds. I thought it might be something fun for him to do. One of my greatest memories when I was his age was spending the afternoon fishing with my dad."

Caitlyn tipped her chin. "I'm sure it was. But you're not his father. I don't want Henry to get wild ideas into his head."

"I understand your concern. Please know that I'll respect your boundaries. I only want the boy to have a little fun, that's all." Logan turned, and they walked the rest of the way in silence.

Upon arriving at the barn, Logan placed his thumb and index finger into his mouth and whistled.

"Cool! Can you teach me to do that?" Henry asked.

Caitlyn pressed her hands to her ears and chuckled. "I'm not sure that's a good idea."

The dogs responded to the whistle. Both the German shepherd and yellow Labrador ran from inside the barn, across the grassy area, to the fence circling the structure. As they peeked through the split-rail, their tales moved back and forth like windshield wipers in a summer rainstorm.

Logan placed his hand on the top of the shepherd's head first. "This is Rocky." Next he introduced the Lab. "And this is Sophie."

"Is it okay for me to pet them?" Henry squeezed his hands together.

Logan turned to Caitlyn. "Sure. If it's okay with your mom, you can go inside."

"Why don't we all do that?" Caitlyn suggested.

Logan led the way and unlocked the gate. He opened the door to the paddock. Both dogs ran to the opening. "Stay," he commanded. The animals obeyed and sat at the gate.

"That's so cool. It's like they understood what you said." Henry continued to observe the dogs.

"I taught them how to obey commands." Logan fished inside the pocket of his jeans and pulled out a treat for Rocky and Sophie. "I try to keep a few in my pocket." He extended his hand to reward each dog.

Logan stepped inside. Caitlyn followed. "Come on in." Logan motioned for Henry to join them, but his earlier excitement appeared to have disappeared.

"They're pretty big." Henry's eyes widened. He kept his arms pinned to his sides and stood rooted in place.

"They won't hurt you. I promise," Logan said in a calm and reassuring tone.

Henry slowly stepped inside the gate before Logan closed it behind him. The dogs remain seated, but their tails continued their rapid movement.

"Don't they like me?" Henry asked.

Caitlyn rested her hand on Henry's shoulder. "Why would you ask that?"

"They aren't coming to me." Henry's lower lip rolled.

Logan squatted in front of Henry. "Do you see their tails moving?"

Henry nodded.

"They are both excited to see you, but they're obeying my command to stay. I've trained them not to move from that position until I give them permission." Unlike some dogs Logan had worked with over the years, Rocky and Sophie had been quick to learn some of the basic commands.

"I wish this little guy would listen that well." Caitlyn ruffled the top of Henry's hair.

Logan stood and clapped his hands. "Okay, guys, you're free." Both animals jumped to their feet and immediately ran to Henry, covering his hands with wet kisses. Henry dropped to the ground, giggling as the dogs shifted from his hands to his face.

Caitlyn moved closer to Logan. Her hair smelled like honeysuckle. "I can't remember the last time I've seen Henry laugh that hard. Thank you for inviting us today."

"It's been my pleasure. You're both welcome to visit the dogs anytime. They're always ready to go for a walk. We've got some fantastic trails that go around the property." Logan loved his quiet time walking outdoors.

Henry lifted his head off the ground while the dogs discovered his ears. "Can we take them for a walk now?"

Logan snuck a quick glance in Caitlyn's direction.

"It couldn't hurt to walk off some more of that delicious meal." Caitlyn rubbed her stomach.

Henry bounced up and down on his toes. "Can we take them down to the pond? I see some ducks down there."

Logan waited for Caitlyn to answer.

"Lead the way. It looks like there's a walking trail that circles the pond," Caitlyn said.

"You're right. There's over a mile of trail around the water. Sophie and Rocky love it. They like to chase the geese and ducks. Let me grab their leashes." Logan jogged inside the barn and returned with two leather straps.

Ten minutes into the walk, Henry held tight to Rocky's leash while the animal forged ahead. Caitlyn did her best to keep pace with Sophie. The animal moved swiftly, her nose buried in the trampled grassy path, eagerly sniffing every scent. Purple wildflowers lined both sides of the trail, providing a splash of color to the otherwise green-and-brown landscape.

"Isn't this cool, Mom? If we lived here, we could do this every day." Henry's eyes were bright with enthusiasm as he daydreamed out loud.

Caitlyn remained silent.

"Look at the ducks! They're swimming closer to the edge." Henry pointed to the water.

"Those are mallards. The one with the glossy green head and white collar is the male, or often referred to as a drake. The other one swimming along his side, streaked with shades of brown, black and buff, is a female." It pleased Logan to see Henry's interest in the birds.

"How do you know so much about ducks?" Henry asked.

"When I was little, back in Virginia, my dad had a boat. We'd spend hours fishing in the pond on our property. He taught me all about the birds and waterfowl we'd see in and around the pond. The female, referred to as a hen, is the one you hear quacking. Male ducks don't quack."

"I never knew that," Caitlyn mused.

Logan watched Henry keep a close eye on the water. "Look at that one over there all alone. How come he looks so different? His face has red bumps on it."

"That's a good observation, Henry. The duck you noticed isn't native to this area. She showed up last spring and set up residency in the pond. It's possible she was someone's pet."

Henry continued to eye the duck. "What kind is it?"

"Donald is a Muscovy."

Caitlyn raised an eyebrow. "You named her Donald?"

Logan laughed. "Well, when I first spotted her, she seemed large. I assumed it was a male, so I named her Donald. Several months after she was here, she built a nest and laid some eggs. By that time, it didn't feel right to change her name." Logan reached down and released Rocky from the leash. The dog took off toward the water. Sophie pulled on her restraint.

Caitlyn turned to Logan. "Is it okay if I let her go?"

"If you don't, she might pull your arm out of the socket." Logan smiled.

Henry jumped up and down. "Can I go down and see Donald close up?"

"Why don't we all go?" Caitlyn reached for Henry's hand.

At the water's edge, Logan took notice of how Henry kept a watchful eye on Donald. He seemed to ignore the other ducks and the larger Canadian geese that circled the pond, honking and flapping their wings.

"Do you like Donald?" Logan asked Henry.

Henry placed his finger to his lip and nodded, and kept his gaze fixed on the duck. "The others stay away from her because she's different," he murmured softly. "Like me." Henry turned and moved from the bank. His enthusiasm for the pond seemed to fade.

Logan spun on his heel to face Caitlyn. His heart raced with worry. "Is he okay?"

A heavy silence hung in the air until a fish splashed in the water. A breeze created a soft rustle of leaves in the trees.

Caitlyn's nod was barely noticeable before she turned and hurried after Henry.

Logan's chest tightened with concern as Caitlyn caught up to her son and knelt in front of him. He strained to hear the conversation, but the murmur of their voices was too soft to discern. Caitlyn took Henry into her arms. Something was troubling him. The incident left Logan with a sense of unease and a nagging feeling that something was terribly wrong.

Chapter Five

Caitlyn stepped inside one of the four bedrooms in Luke Beckett's cottage-like house.

A colorful mural of a rodeo with a bull rider in the ring filled one wall. The two adjacent windows had curtains covered with pictures of horses. Caitlyn laughed to herself. Luke had definitely had a say in decorating the room.

Not paying for an expensive motel eased her mind somewhat, but it couldn't erase the look on Henry's face yesterday at the pond. Her heart pounded as she recalled his meltdown. The poor boy had barely mustered the energy to climb onto the top bunk in one of the kid's rooms, where he remained sound asleep.

It was still early. The soft light of a new day filtered through the curtains. Maybe she'd let him sleep a little longer while she spent some time planning the hours ahead. Caitlyn tiptoed toward the door and reached for the handle. The aroma of the freshly brewed coffee she'd prepared earlier drifted into the bedroom, inviting her to the kitchen.

"Can we go to the pond and visit Donald after breakfast?" Henry sat up in the bed and rubbed his eyes.

A part of Caitlyn had hoped that after Henry had a good night of sleep, he would have forgotten about the duck. But she knew better. Henry saw himself in Donald. With her red, bumpy face the complete opposite of the beautiful and iridescent mallard ducks, Donald was different. Caitlyn tried to convince her son that he was special, not different. But Henry felt like he didn't fit in with his friends. Each time he'd experienced a seizure in front of his classmates, it became harder for Henry to believe his mother. Yesterday, while Caitlyn watched the other ducks exclude Donald, she understood why Henry felt an attachment.

"I thought you were still sleeping."

Dressed in his superhero pajamas, Henry climbed down the ladder as if he did it every day.

"Be careful, sweetie," Caitlyn cautioned Henry.

"This is easy. Can we get a bunk bed in my room?"

A few seconds ticked by. Given her current financial situation, Caitlyn questioned if she and Henry would still have a home once they returned to Wyoming. Last night, she'd received a text message from her landlord asking her to call him. Until she had a better idea on the timeline of the repairs, she planned to try her best to avoid talking with him. "We'll see."

Henry shook his head and frowned. "That means no."

Caitlyn moved across the bedroom and drew the curtains. She squinted as a stream of bright morning light radiated through the window. "Not necessarily. We have a lot to take care of here first." Caitlyn's heart rate increased.

"What about Donald? Can we go see her? That doesn't cost any money."

Caitlyn didn't want Henry to start his day with two disappointments. She glanced at her watch. Logan mentioned a training session he and his brother Jake had this morning. After, Logan planned to get started on the house. "We'll have to make it a quick visit. Mr. Logan and his crew are going to begin repairs today."

"At Last Dollar?" Henry asked.

Caitlyn blinked rapidly. "What are you talking about?"

"Our house—I saw the sign. It's on Last Dollar Road. Isn't that a cool name?"

With everything going on, the street name of her childhood home had slipped her mind. No surprise there. Over the years, it had been easier for Caitlyn to push aside the negative memories. The only problem was that before her parents' accident, there'd been a lot of wonderful memories. She chuckled at the coincidence. Henry's name described the home perfectly. The way things were going, it would probably take her last dollar to get it ready to sell.

Caitlyn reached out and ran her hand across Henry's cheek. He always liked to name things. Moving from one foster home to another, Henry had slept in a lot of beds. After she'd signed the adoption papers, as she'd tucked him into his bed that night, he'd told Caitlyn he'd never felt this way in a bed. The next day, he'd told her he'd named his bed "Mr. Cozy." After that, he'd named her SUV "Lucy." Caitlyn smiled at the memory and laughed. "I don't think I could have come up with a more perfect name for the house."

Caitlyn extended her hand. "Let's get you cleaned up and dressed. I'll make some toast and fix you a bowl of cereal. I'd like to go into town and pick up some additional cleaning supplies." This morning, while logging into her online banking, she'd noticed a deposit for her monthly cash reward from her credit card. The money would come in handy for her trip to the store.

"What about Donald? You said we could go see her."

"We'll stop by the pond on our way back from town. Go wash your face and put on the clothes I laid on the vanity in the bathroom. I'm going to get breakfast ready."

"Yes!" Henry ran to the bathroom at the end of the hall.

Caitlyn watched until he slammed the door closed. If seeing Donald made her son smile, then she'd have to put aside her worries. As long as Henry spent time with the duck when Logan wasn't around, she could avoid answering questions like he'd asked yesterday. Caitlyn appreciated Logan's concern for Henry. But sharing the reason for Henry's attachment to Donald would only open up the possibilities of more questions. Keeping Henry's health and her dire financial situation private was a priority.

Forty-five minutes later, they were ready to head out. With Henry securely buckled in the booster seat of the SUV, Caitlyn was prepared to begin a long day. She pushed the ignition button but the engine didn't start. A second attempt gave the same result. This time, she sent up a silent prayer before trying it. Still nothing. A pain throbbed in her left temple.

"Why aren't we going?" Henry called out from behind.

Caitlyn was asking the same thing until she remembered canceling the five-thousand-mile checkup with the car dealership. Prior to learning about her inheritance, she had scheduled service for the vehicle. The same day she'd made the appointment, came a surprise bill from Henry's trip to the emergency room the prior month. She'd added finding an independent mechanic who charged less to her list of things to do and canceled the service appointment. After, she'd gone online and paid one fourth of the balance owed to the hospital. "The car won't start."

"Maybe you should call those people that come to help?" Henry suggested.

Something else Caitlyn had canceled while evaluating her monthly budget was the auto club membership. She'd never used it last year. It was money down the drain. Or so she'd thought. When the renewal notice arrived in the mail along with a hefty increase in the annual fee, she'd opted not to renew and shredded the notice. She released a heavy breath. "That's not an option since I canceled my membership."

"Because of me?"

Caitlyn looked into the rearview mirror. "What makes you say something like that, sweetie?"

"All the bills are because of my epilepsy."

Caitlyn tried her best to protect Henry from knowing about her financial struggles, but as he grew older, he became more perceptive. It hadn't helped that recently he'd overheard her on the phone with their landlord. She'd explained the medical debt and promised to do her best to catch up on the rent. Two days later, he'd heard her talking with the billing department at Henry's doctor's office. "No, my canceling the service had nothing to do with you, sweetie. It made little sense to renew since I never used it the year before." Caitlyn eyed Henry lovingly in the rearview mirror.

"I sure wish we had it now. I really wanted to see Donald."

"Donald isn't going anywhere. You'll have plenty of time to visit her."

"It looks like we aren't going anywhere either," Henry sighed.

Henry's words sounded more like a teenager's than a seven-year-old's. He was growing up much too fast for her.

"We'll be on our way before you know it." Caitlyn unbuckled her seat belt, popped the hood and exited the vehicle. She knew a little about cars. Thanks to the internet, she'd recently saved herself over sixty dollars by watching a video on how to do an oil change. It was a messy job.

But using the extra money to cover the water bill provided breathing room on her budget, not to mention the satisfaction she'd gotten from doing the job herself.

"Are you going to fix it?" Henry removed his belt and jumped down to the ground. He rounded the SUV and joined Caitlyn at her side. "I can help you." He looked up and squinted into the sunlight.

Caitlyn looked down at Henry. "You just being here helps, sweetie. I have a feeling the car probably needs a new battery."

Henry's eyes brightened. "My Game Boy is in the house. It has a battery. I'll get it for you."

Caitlyn laughed and placed her hand on Henry's shoulder. His heart was always in the right place. Caitlyn was proud of the little boy who was too quickly growing into a young man. "Your Game Boy takes a different type of battery, but I appreciate your generous offer."

Henry chewed on his lower lip and studied the open hood. "Maybe you should call Mr. Logan. He probably knows a lot about cars. I'm sure he can fix it fast. Then I can go visit Donald. Maybe Mr. Logan can come with us? He knows a lot about ducks."

Since Caitlyn's arrival in Bluebell Canyon, Logan had already gone above and beyond to help her get the property ready to put on the market. She'd like to believe it was out of the goodness of Logan's heart, but her experience with men had made her suspicious. Logan was probably only interested in taking possession of the land she'd agreed to sell.

"Come on, Mom. Call him. I think Mr. Logan knows a lot more about cars than Mr. Jeffrey did. He couldn't fix anything. Remember when the wheel came loose on my scooter? He didn't even know a screwdriver from a hammer." Henry rolled his eyes.

Caitlyn stifled her laugh. Henry was right. Her ex-boyfriend had been all about the money. Creating wealth by refinancing homes was his top priority. If something broke, you hired someone to fix it. Learning how to do menial tasks wasn't worth his time. Toward the end of their relationship, Jeffrey had resented Henry because of his medical condition. It had consumed her attention and the one thing she'd learned about Jeffrey was that he enjoyed being the center of attention. Henry had sensed the resentment, which had made it easier for Caitlyn to deal with the breakup. In the end, she'd repaired Henry's scooter herself.

As much as Caitlyn hated to, she really had no other choice but to call Logan for help. She and Henry could hike over to Last Dollar, but that would waste time she couldn't spare. How would it look if she showed up late when so many kindhearted people were offering their time and help? She pulled in a deep breath and took out her cell phone.

To say it surprised Logan to receive a call from Caitlyn asking for help would be an understatement. It was the last thing he'd expected from Caitlyn, who seemed fiercely independent and didn't need anyone's help, especially a man's. Perhaps someone had betrayed her in the past, causing her to be cautious and not rely on anyone. Or maybe it was because she'd lost her parents early in life. As tempted as he was to learn more about this intriguing woman, Logan refused to pry into her personal life. Keeping things on a business level was the safest way to protect his heart. Yet despite his curiosity, he couldn't help but feel a sense of duty and determination to be there for her and Henry in any way he could.

Logan headed up Luke's driveway and spotted Caitlyn in front of her SUV with her journal in hand. She wore faded blue jeans, a green-and-yellow top, along with a tan cowboy hat, and boots that gleamed. He couldn't ignore the fact that she looked beautiful.

Caitlyn never looked up as his pickup approached. She scribbled inside the pages of her journal. Henry busied himself twirling with his arms extended, occasionally losing his balance while staring up at the sky.

Logan parked and stepped out of the truck.

"Mr. Logan!" Henry ran toward him while his mother finished her thought and closed the journal.

"Hey, buddy. How'd you sleep last night?"

"Great! I love the bunk bed. If I had one in my room, I'd never argue with Mom about my bedtime."

"I had a feeling you'd like the bed." Logan patted Henry's shoulder.

Henry's smile quickly faded.

"What's wrong?" Logan asked.

"I'm kind of bummed out. The car won't start. I wanted to go see Donald before we go to Last Dollar." Henry frowned.

Logan scratched his head and turned in Caitlyn's direction. "I understand going to visit Donald, but I'm a little unclear about the last dollar part."

Caitlyn rolled her eyes. "He's named the house. He always likes to give everything a name."

Logan laughed and ruffled the top of his head. "I get it now. The house is on Last Dollar Road. That's pretty creative."

Caitlyn placed the journal on the roof of her SUV before turning to face Logan. "As much as the house is going to cost me to get it ready to sell, I think Henry's name describes it perfectly."

If Caitlyn would let go of her stubborn ways, the kind-hearted people in Bluebell Canyon could prevent her from spending money on repairs. "Well, right now there are ten volunteers working hard to put a new roof on your house."

Caitlyn stood speechless. Her arched brow carried surprise.

Logan had a feeling his change of plans about the roof might upset Caitlyn. As she stood wringing her hands together, he knew his assumption had been correct.

"I didn't give the go-ahead for a new roof. It was my understanding that you would make repairs to the existing structure."

Logan offered an understanding nod. "I know what we discussed, but George, the inspector, didn't feel the integrity of the roof was worth repairing. A new roof would make better use of the donated materials."

Caitlyn shook her head and kicked the tip of her boot into the ground. "I can't cover the cost of a new roof along with fixing all the other problems with the house. It's just not in my budget."

"You probably have your journal filled with funds allocated for the repairs that need to be addressed." He tilted his head toward the roof of the SUV. "But whether you repair the roof or do a complete replacement, it won't cost you anything. The men have donated their time, along with the material, out of the kindness of their hearts. They want to help you. Besides, selling a home in pristine condition versus patchwork repairs can benefit the community in the long run. It can raise the comparable sales in the area. If anyone sells their home, your sales price could increase their property value."

"I don't feel comfortable being the town charity case," Caitlyn said.

"Relax, Mom. I think it's pretty cool people want to help you. It's like Mrs. Wilson taught us in Bible school. She said you have to be good to your neighbor. It's what God wants us to do."

Logan watched as the tension appeared to subside.

Caitlyn's shoulders relaxed. A smile traced her lips. "You're right, sweetie, that's exactly what God wants us to do. Thanks for reminding me."

"Now that we have that straightened out, let me look." Logan rubbed his hands against his pant legs and stepped closer to the open hood.

Caitlyn summarized what had happened when she'd tried to start the vehicle. Logan tinkered underneath the hood before attempting to get the vehicle going. He agreed it was most likely the battery. "I'll get my jumper cables. If it is the battery and we get it started, I'll follow you over to Last Dollar and then run out and get you a replacement. It's easy to install, so I can pop it in and then we can get to work on a few of the interior projects."

"What about Donald? Mom said we could visit with her." Henry gave Logan a hopeful look.

"If it's okay with your mother, you can ride along with me to get the new battery. On the way back, we can stop and say hello to Donald if you'd like."

Henry bounced on his toes. "Can I, Mom? Please!"

"Let's wait until Mr. Logan determines what's wrong with the car. If it is the battery, we can all go together to pick it up so I can pay for it myself. Plus, I wanted to pick up a few cleaning supplies. If there's enough time after, we can make a quick visit with Donald. Remember, we have a lot of work to do if we want to get back home."

"But I'm not in a hurry to go home. I like it here. Why can't we keep Last Dollar house and just live there? I like this town. Plus, Mr. Logan and Donald are here," Henry pleaded.

For the second time in five minutes, Logan watched Caitlyn's shoulders stiffen. It was obvious she wanted no part of making her childhood home a place for her and Henry.

"Let me get those cables." Logan spun on his heel and headed to his truck. The longer those two stayed in Bluebell, the more of a challenge Caitlyn would have with Henry.

An hour and a half later, Logan found himself at the pond once again with Caitlyn and Henry. He'd wanted to bring the dogs along for Henry, but Caitlyn had insisted this would be a quick visit. She was eager to get to work.

"Thank you again for taking me to pick up the battery. That's an enormous weight off my mind." Caitlyn gave Logan a warm smile, causing his pulse to tick up a few beats.

"It was no big deal. Glad I could help." Assisting others came naturally to Logan, but it also served as a reminder of the one time he hadn't been there for the person he'd loved the most. His fiancée had needed him, and he hadn't been there. The guilt gnawed at him every day, every moment.

"It surprised me how inexpensive a new battery could be." Caitlyn tossed him a questioning eye.

"Let's just say I'm a long-time customer of Gary's shop. I've done a few favors for him, so he was just paying it forward."

"Look!" Henry pointed out to the water. "A couple of gigantic birds are swimming toward Donald. We saw those before. Aren't they from Canada or some place? Maybe they want to be friends with her."

Logan looked out across the pond. "They're Canadian geese."

As the geese drew closer to Donald, their honking grew louder and more aggressive. They spread their wings and puffed up their chests. Donald continued to paddle, unfazed by the commotion surrounding her.

Henry kept his gaze fixed on the water.

The geese were relentless. They formed a semicircle around Donald and honked in unison.

"Why are they doing that?" Henry asked.

Logan slipped his hands into his back pockets. "This is their pond. Geese aren't always welcoming to other types of waterfowl. They know she's different."

Donald continued to paddle around, occasionally flapping her wings in defiance.

Henry stomped his foot into the dirt. "They're being so mean. Can't we help her?"

"Donald can take care of herself." Logan rested his hand on Henry's shoulder.

Henry continued to study Donald's reaction until the geese finally won the battle and Donald swam away, defeated and alone. "I wish we could build Donald her own pond and bring other ducks like her to live with her."

Logan looked down at Henry, pleased. "That sounds like a good idea. Maybe if everything works out with the sale of the property, I can do that."

Henry's head cocked to one side. "Really? That would be so cool!" He turned to his mother. "If Mr. Logan builds a new pond for Donald, can we come back and visit?"

Caitlyn tossed Logan a look of displeasure about his idea of building a new home for Donald and a few friends.

"I think we'll have to wait and see what happens, buddy. I could always email you some pictures and videos," Logan offered.

Henry looked down at the ground. "That's not really the same. I don't understand why we can't just move here. You could have your school here, couldn't you, Mom? There's lots of land."

Logan was unclear of what Henry was alluding to. He looked at Caitlyn but she avoided his gaze, staring at the grass.

"Don't you think so, Mom?"

Logan was relieved when Henry pushed his mother. Caitlyn did her best to keep her life in Wyoming to herself, but he wanted to know more about her.

"With all the property around Last Dollar, you could get more horses. Then maybe more girls could sign up for your class." Henry appeared excited by his own suggestion.

It was then Logan remembered. His brother had mentioned Caitlyn's dream to start a school to teach barrel racing.

"Owning more horses requires a bigger expense, sweetie. It's not as simple as just having the property to board them," Caitlyn explained to Henry.

"Yeah, but wouldn't you make more money if you had a bigger class?"

Logan concealed a grin with his left hand. Henry might be seven years old, but he had a pretty good business head on his shoulders.

"If we moved here, I could help you more. I promise. Please, Mom."

Caitlyn rubbed her hand down the front of her jeans. "I think we need to discuss this another time." She glanced at Henry.

"Your mom is right, buddy." Logan noted the time on his watch. "We better get going. It's past the lunch hour. I still need to install the new car battery and then we've got a lot of work to do."

"I don't want to leave Donald. She'll be lonely without me." Henry gazed out at the water.

"Donald will be fine. Don't worry. If we don't get to Last Dollar, everyone's going to think we're goofing off. Knowing those guys, they've probably already finished putting on the new roof." Logan looked at Caitlyn and grinned. This time, she returned his gesture with a smile. But this one was different, and it ignited warmth in him like a cozy fireplace on a cold winter night. For a moment, Logan felt he could brave any storm as long as he had Caitlyn's smile to light his way.

Chapter Six

Caitlyn didn't like this one bit. But she had to admit the mix of experienced carpenters and enthusiastic volunteers brought new life to the sagging and dilapidated roof. Sounds of hammers and saws echoed across the open field. Men worked steadily, hoisting heavy bundles of shingles onto their shoulders and carrying them up to the roof while others nailed them down in place.

The sense of camaraderie among the men as they laughed and joked with each other captivated Caitlyn. "What they're doing is amazing." She turned to Logan, who stood by her side.

"It's great, isn't it?" Logan waved at his neighbors. "They're standing in the gap. It's what being a part of a community is about."

Caitlyn's eyes welled with inexplicable tears. Why was she so emotional watching these men?

"Are you okay?" Logan asked.

Get a grip.

This reaction was so unlike Caitlyn. Her decision to be independent and to not rely on others had worked fine throughout her life. She'd let down her guard with her ex and look where that had gotten her. Yet, as she observed the progress being made, even though there was still much work to be done, she knew doing it on her own wasn't possible. If she wanted to get back to Wyoming and mend her broken life, maybe setting aside her ego was the only option. "I'm fine. It's all just a little overwhelming."

"Mom! Come inside and see what all they've done," Henry called from the front porch.

Logan placed his hand on Caitlyn's lower back. "I told you they'd have a full day of work conquered by the time we got here. They are a determined bunch. Let's go check it out."

Caitlyn climbed the front steps and rubbed the wetness underneath each eye with her index finger. She'd never met such generous people in her life. Once inside the home, the smell of freshly squeezed lemons teased her senses. "It looks so much brighter in here." She scanned the parlor, thinking that first a coat of fresh paint had brought additional light into the room. But upon further inspection, the original beige color that had been there when she'd moved out remained, only more faded and dingy.

"A few of the ladies from church came by early this morning, loaded down with sponges and squeegees to clean the windows." Nelson stepped forward, wiping the sweat from his forehead with a handkerchief he had pulled from his back pocket. He unscrewed the cap from a bottle of water in his hand and took a long swig. "They thought it would be easier for us to see what needs to be done once they scrubbed away years of grime and dirt that had accumulated on the windowpanes."

"They did a fantastic job." Caitlyn looked around the room. "The place desperately needs a new paint job," Caitlyn added.

"I can help paint!" Henry offered.

Caitlyn eyed the black outlines going up the staircase

where family pictures had covered the walls. The first outline was where her parents' wedding picture had once hung.

"After we get the floors done in here, we'll take care of the paint. Don't worry," Logan reassured Caitlyn.

"Jeb came by at the crack of dawn with the new hot water heater. I've got it installed, so you're good to go. You can take as many long, hot showers as you'd like." Nelson drained the last gulp from his bottle.

Logan glanced at Caitlyn. "Did you hear that? Something else you can check off from your list. Everything is moving right along, so you can relax. You and Henry will be back in Wyoming before you know it."

Nelson cleared his throat. "Unfortunately, you won't be able to check off the wiring issue today."

Caitlyn's joy over the water tank slumped.

"Why is that?" Logan asked.

"Lester came by earlier this morning. Becky's mother is ill, so they're driving to Memphis. He hopes to be back by Friday, but nothing is definite," Nelson explained.

Caitlyn was sorry to hear about Lester's mother-in-law and sent up a silent prayer. This wasn't good. "Maybe I better hire someone."

"I know you're in a hurry to get back to Wyoming, but it might be in your best interest to wait for Lester. If this turns out to be a bigger job than he expects, hiring an electrician could eat away at your budget," Logan said.

As much as Caitlyn wanted to hurry and get the house sold, she had to be realistic. Logan was right. Given the age of the home, she had to be prepared that the entire place might need new wiring. That was a cost she could never afford without maxing out her emergency credit card. She'd opened that line of credit after Henry's diagnosis—just in case. "I suppose waiting a few more days won't hurt. In the meantime, there are other projects to address." Caitlyn's eyes locked on Logan.

He rested his hand on Caitlyn's arm. "You've made the right decision. In the long run, waiting on Lester will save you a lot of money."

"The good news is, before he left town, Lester contacted his fire restoration buddy, Jacob. He said Jacob and his crew will be out tomorrow afternoon to begin the cleanup of the attic," Nelson confirmed.

Caitlyn considered Nelson's report and gazed out the window of the farmhouse. The vibrant greens and golden yellows of the rolling field sparked memories of her childhood. For a moment, a twinge of sadness filled Caitlyn's heart. There wouldn't be any hot showers or leisurely evenings spent on a renovated porch swing with Henry. She shook off the thought. Bluebell wasn't her home. Not since the death of her parents. There were too many sad memories buried inside this old house.

Nelson glanced at his watch. "If you two are ready to get to work, Charles dropped off several gallons of paint for the main bedroom. You can get started up there, if you'd like."

Caitlyn chewed her lip. "What about the flooring in the room? It seemed in rough shape."

"There was nothing that a few nails and a little sanding couldn't fix. After that, the ladies polished the wood. It looks fantastic. We thought you'd want to get that room finished up first, in case you planned to stay in the house, but it sounds like you'll be heading back to Wyoming soon." Nelson paused and glanced between Logan and Caitlyn. "Then again, you might change your mind. I can't count the number of folks who visited Bluebell over the years but ended up making this wonderful town their home. You and your son might be next."

"That would be awesome!" Henry cheered and looked up at Nelson. "I sure hope my mom changes her mind."

Nelson smiled at Henry. "I hope so, too. Why don't you run back to the kitchen? School had an early release today, so there are a few kids devouring a plate of homemade cookies my wife made. After they finish their snack, they're going to help clean up the garden and the barn."

Henry turned to his mother. "Can I?"

Caitlyn hesitated for a moment.

"Don't worry. The children will have some adult supervision." Nelson rested his hand on Caitlyn's arm. "He'll be fine."

Nelson was a kind man. It was as though he'd read her mind. "Have fun." Caitlyn nodded at Henry. "You haven't had lunch yet, so don't eat too many cookies."

"Thelma also fried a ton of chicken, so help yourself, son." Nelson extended the offer before turning to Caitlyn and Logan. Henry took off in a hurry. "Maybe you two should eat before you get started upstairs."

Logan rubbed his stomach. "Let's go grab some lunch. I'm starving." He nudged Caitlyn's arm.

"That sounds good to me." Caitlyn's stomach had been growling for the last hour.

"The fellas set up a couple of picnic tables in the backyard," Nelson said.

Logan patted Nelson on the shoulder. "You thought of everything. Thanks, bud."

Nelson focused his attention back on the loose floorboards as Caitlyn followed Logan to the kitchen.

Minutes later, Caitlyn sat at a rickety table nestled beneath the giant weeping willow tree. Henry had grabbed a chicken leg and headed to the barn. Apparently, one kid had told him there were a couple of stray cats inside. Logan offered to bring out the food and asked that she grab a spot to sit down. She looked up at the sprawling branches rustling in the breeze and draping down around her like a protective canopy.

Caitlyn inhaled a deep breath and relaxed for the first time since discovering her car wouldn't start. She scanned the property filled with gorgeous blue and white columbine. Not much about the landscape had changed since she was a young girl, but she couldn't say the same about herself. The carefree child who used to sip a cold beverage on the porch swing with her daddy no longer existed.

As much as she tried to focus on her blessings, Caitlyn couldn't shake the feeling of despair that had settled over her like a dark cloud. She was on the verge of losing her home and, with each day that passed, the weight of her financial burden threatened to drown her. It left her feeling like she was treading water in the middle of the ocean with nothing but a deflated raft. But then, at her lowest moments, she'd think of Henry. He was the best thing that had ever happened to her.

Despite the mounting obstacles, Caitlyn had no other choice but to continue working hard and get the house ready to sell. It was the only way to keep a roof over their heads and pay off her debt, and then maybe she could focus on her dream of expanding her business.

But convincing Henry that they didn't belong in Bluebell was becoming more difficult. Caitlyn couldn't deny the allure of the small town with its friendly people. But the costs of moving there permanently would send her further into debt, and she couldn't bear the thought of putting her son's future in jeopardy.

Caitlyn's head whipped around at the sound of the screen door slamming. Her heart rate quickened as she caught sight of Logan. His muscles rippled beneath his white T-shirt as he juggled two plates of food, piled high with fried chicken, mashed potatoes, corn on the cob and biscuits.

The flutter in her stomach caught her off guard when she met his warm, inviting smile. Caitlyn couldn't deny the attraction. She tried to shake off the feeling and focus on the task at hand, but she couldn't help but steal another glance in Logan's direction.

Logan carefully placed the plates on the table.

"Should I run inside for some drinks?" Caitlyn asked.

"Nope, I've got them right here." Logan reached behind his back. "I hope you like grape?" He grinned and pulled two cans of soda from each back pocket.

The memory of sipping icy grape soda on the porch swing with her father played through her mind. "It's my favorite." She accepted his offering and popped the top. The carbonated fizz tickled her nose.

"Mine, too." Logan opened his beverage, took a drink, and placed the can on the table. "Hold on one second. I'll be right back." He spun on his heel and sprinted back inside the house.

Caitlyn eyed the extra-crispy piece of chicken on her plate. Her stomach rumbled in response to the delicious aroma, but she waited for Logan to return.

Moments later, Logan strolled to the table with a water glass filled with freshly picked vibrant blue forget-me-nots. He set the glass between their two plates. "I thought you'd like these while we enjoy our meal."

Caitlyn's heart warmed. "Thank you for this." She traced her finger down the side of the glass. "That's very thoughtful of you. When I was a little girl, I used to pick forget-me-nots for my mother. She told me they reminded her of me." Caitlyn remained quiet and stared out over the open countryside. She glanced at Logan, who appeared to be saying a prayer over his food.

Logan lifted his head. He picked up his napkin and placed it on his lap. "I saw you noticing the flowers out front earlier," he admitted.

Caitlyn couldn't ignore the pang of sadness. Maybe if she was at a different place in her life, Logan could be the prince she had dreamed of as a little girl. But the pain and suffering she had endured earlier in life had left her feeling lost and alone, trapped in the wilderness of her own heart. Caitlyn yearned for the love that would make her feel whole again, but the scars from her past ran too deep.

Caitlyn leaned forward and held her stomach. "I don't remember the last time I've eaten such an enormous meal."

"You really packed it away," he teased. Logan liked a woman with a healthy appetite.

Caitlyn reached over and gave Logan's arm a playful swat. "Thanks a lot."

Amusement tugged at his mouth. "I'm only joking. It's nice to see a person enjoy their meal." Logan ran his eyes over her empty plate. "You really did a number on that corn cob."

She dabbed the napkin against her lips. "It's always been a favorite of mine. But you didn't do so bad yourself. You looked like a beaver going to town on the last tree standing by a lake."

Logan laughed and glanced at the gnawed cob. "You got me there. I saw some of Nellie's famous homemade brownies in the kitchen—if you're interested." Logan's brow arched.

"Honestly, I can't eat another bite, but I'll take a rain check for later." Caitlyn pushed a strand of hair blowing in the gentle breeze away from her face. "I don't know how you expect me to paint after this big lunch. I feel like I could curl up and take a nap."

While enjoying their meal, Logan couldn't ignore how Caitlyn's serious demeanor had softened. A more playful and easygoing side had blossomed. He found himself drawn to her even more, both intellectually and physically. He couldn't deny the attraction he felt. Despite knowing Caitlyn valued her privacy, Logan wanted to learn more about her and the life she lived in Wyoming. "I hope you don't mind me asking, but I'm curious about your school. I'd love to hear more about it."

A peaceful smile appeared. Caitlyn's hazel eyes shimmered in the sunlight. "If there's one thing I'll talk nonstop about, it's my barrel racing school. It was a dream I had for many years. In fact, I'm sure your brother got sick of listening to me ramble on about it." She chuckled.

"Back in the day, when I asked Luke about you, he mentioned how excited you were about your new venture. But he never said he was tired of hearing about it. He was proud of you," Logan told her.

Caitlyn tilted her head and her eyes grew bigger. "You asked Luke about me? I didn't think you knew I existed." She gave a nervous laugh and squirmed on the bench.

Logan remembered how his heart had rattled inside his chest the first time he'd met Caitlyn. She'd worn tan, form-fitting riding pants that had hugged her athletic physique in all the right places. A white button up shirt highlighted her hazel eyes. The high-heeled Western boots and the dark brown cowboy hat had completed her attire. She was a knockout. He'd realized then that there was more to her than beauty after she'd taken first place in the women's championship barrel racing competition. He swallowed the lump in his throat. "Oh, trust me. I noticed you. How could any man with a pulse not?"

Caitlyn tipped her chin down and her face flushed.

"I'm sorry. I didn't mean to embarrass you. My mother taught me to always be truthful—especially to a lady."

The sound of hammers pounding nails and whirling power tools echoed through the air.

"So tell me about the school." Logan needed to get his focus off of Caitlyn's stunning good looks. Or at least to try to.

"Over the years, I had a few injuries. Thanks to the aging process, with each injury came longer and more difficult recovery times. During those periods when I had to take a break from competition, I kept a journal to plot ideas to achieve my dream of opening a school. For six months, I mentored a few girls in between competitions." Caitlyn's eyes lit up with excitement. "I loved to see their enthusiasm for the sport, especially when I taught them something they never believed they could do. I realized that was the path I needed to follow. Once I had my plan in place, I announced my retirement and adopted Henry."

"That's quite a story. But you left out one of the best parts." Logan placed his elbows on the table and leaned forward.

Caitlyn grinned widely. "No. I don't believe I did. Adopting Henry was the best part of it all." Her face was a canvas of emotion while her voice conveyed tenderness.

"I don't doubt that. What I should have said was you left out the best part of your career. The recognition your school has received is impressive. Being voted number one in the country is a major achievement. That's incredible. I'm proud of you." Logan's eyes sparkled with admiration.

"How did you know about that?" Caitlyn asked.

Busted. He'd have to come clean. He put his hands up. "Okay, I confess. After we first met, I followed your career for a while, but then life got busy. Until last night, it had been a long time since I went sleuthing. It's amazing what you can find on the internet." Logan's face felt like he'd just stepped inside a sauna. The last thing he wanted was for Caitlyn to think he was some sort of creepy stalker who trolled the web late into the night.

Caitlyn straightened her shoulders. "As long as we're making confessions, I've done a little sleuthing myself and searched for your name online a few times." Her cheeks blushed when their eyes briefly connected.

Logan laughed. "You're just saying that so I don't feel like a silly high school boy."

"I promise." Caitlyn put up her right hand. "I know you have a few service training accolades to be proud of yourself."

Logan ran his finger down the side of his soda can. "I can't take all the credit. My brothers play a huge role in the success of our school."

Caitlyn nodded. "I'm sure you work just as hard as they do. What I was referring to was the article I read about the dog you rescued and trained for the little girl who lost both of her eyes in that tragic accident. What you did was incredible."

Logan preferred to stay out of the limelight, but he understood that as a business owner, sometimes he had to step out of the shadow and into the light. "Thank you. When a neighbor of the little girl, who was a reporter from a Denver newspaper, called me for an interview, I was hesitant at first. But the reporter was persistent. He shared with me how he had witnessed the remarkable transformation the dog had brought to the little girl's life and her family's.

When I realized telling the story could help others understand the power of service dogs, I agreed to the interview."

Caitlyn brushed away a tear that ran down her cheek. "I can't imagine how grateful her parents must have been. What a magnificent gift you gave to the family."

"Seeing the impact the animal had on the family was actually a gift to me," Logan shared. But deep down, Logan couldn't help but feel that he didn't deserve it. He had failed to protect the person he'd loved the most.

"I'm sure it was. You should be proud," she stated.

Logan wanted to share more with Caitlyn, but he thought it was best to keep it to himself.

After losing Melody, Logan had made two promises to God. One was to spend the rest of his life training dogs. He wanted to make a positive impact on as many lives as possible. His second promise was to use some of the property he'd been leasing from Martha to establish a rescue organization. Logan's love for dogs was the driving force behind his dream to start the organization. But a part of him hoped that by rescuing these dogs it would somehow lessen the pain and guilt of not being able to rescue his fiancée.

Chapter Seven

Early Saturday morning, Caitlyn eased her SUV into the gravel lot in front of Garrison's Mercantile. She parked in an open spot and removed the list she'd prepared earlier of ingredients to bake her mother's German chocolate cake. Whenever Caitlyn was nervous, her antidote was to bake. A text message from her landlord late yesterday had her rattled. She'd gotten up before dawn and downed half a pot of coffee before rousting Henry out of bed.

"The sign says closed." Henry poked his head up from behind his Game Boy and studied the front of the market.

Caitlyn eyed her son in the rearview mirror. He'd obviously decided against picking up a hairbrush this morning. She glanced at the time on the dashboard and reached inside her purse. "They should open up any minute. Here, take my comb and run it through your hair before we go inside?"

Henry followed his mother's instructions and combed his unruly hair. "Why did we have to come so early? I didn't even get to watch the Saturday cartoons."

Poor Henry had to suffer the consequences of his mother's nervous tendency to bake following a surprise invitation yesterday. After she and Henry had spent all day at Last Dollar, Logan had stopped by to check on the attic. Lester and his wife were still in Memphis, tending to Becky's mother, but

Lester had wanted Logan to make sure the fire restoration project was being addressed. After Logan had conducted his inspection, he'd invited Caitlyn and Henry to a Memorial Day cookout tomorrow.

If Caitlyn hadn't been so exhausted from removing the grungy wallpaper from the kitchen, she might have declined the invitation. But she was so tired she'd been unable to come up with a fast excuse. Of course, Henry had been so excited by the offer, he'd accepted on her behalf immediately. "I told you I need to get the ingredients to bake a cake to take to the town cookout tomorrow."

"Oh, yeah. That's the party at Mr. Logan's brother's house that's making you nervous." Henry pushed the bill of his hat up from his eyes. "Do you think there will be a lot of kids there?"

"I'm not nervous. There's just a lot on my mind." According to Logan, the party was an annual event held the Sunday before Memorial Day, immediately following church service. This year, it was to be hosted by his brother Jake and his wife, Olivia. "I'm sure there will be a lot of children attending. I believe Mr. Jake has three kids."

"That will be fun. But what about today? It won't take you all day to bake a cake. It's Saturday. We always do something fun at home on Saturday," Henry pleaded.

Henry was right. Following the adoption, Caitlyn had made sure that Saturdays were their day. No matter how busy she was with teaching or managing the business, she always set aside the day for Henry. Each week, she would allow Henry to make up the itinerary for the day. Caitlyn had to admit, putting a squiggly worm on a fishing hook wasn't at the top of her list of things to do. But as long as she was with Henry and he was happy, she really didn't care what they did. "Let's get what we need in the store, and then we'll make a plan for the day."

Henry unbuckled his seat belt. "Okay. Maybe we can go see Rocky and Sophie today? Mr. Logan might let us take them to the pond. Then we can see Donald, too. Or maybe we can go fishing like he talked about."

With Logan being so involved with the repairs on Last Dollar, it was increasingly more difficult to limit the time Henry spent with Logan. Although his heart was in the right place, Caitlyn feared too much time with Logan couldn't be a good thing for her son. If she was being honest, it probably wasn't such a good thing for her either. Logan's handsome good looks were consuming more of her thoughts lately. It didn't help either that since their private picnic last Monday, Logan was giving Caitlyn fresh forget-me-nots each time he came to the house. It was a sweet and kind gesture, but not the best way for her to maintain her focus on getting the repairs done, selling the house, and leaving town.

"Why don't we see what the day brings?" Caitlyn exited the vehicle and opened the back door.

Henry bounded to the ground and pointed. "Look, that place over there has a ball pit outside."

Caitlyn glanced down the street. As far as she could see down the sidewalk, each lamppost had a flower basket filled with colorful petunias. She spotted what had captured Henry's attention. The Hummingbird Café. It appeared to be a quaint bistro-type establishment. A place she'd like to spend a lazy Saturday afternoon with her journal and a cup of strong coffee. It probably wasn't the best environment for a rambunctious little boy. Then again, the ball pit could keep Henry occupied. "Maybe we can go there for lunch sometime."

"Or we could go there?" Henry shouted and turned

his attention across the street. "They probably have good pizza."

"With a name like Mr. Pepperoni, I have to agree with you. Let me take care of my errands. After that, we could explore the town a little and maybe get a pizza for lunch." Making plans with Henry was settling Caitlyn's nerves about accepting Logan's invitation. After all, it was only a cookout.

Caitlyn locked the door of the SUV and glanced at the front window of the store. She noticed the Closed sign had been flipped and now read Open. "Let's go inside." She took Henry's hand and they climbed the steps of the clapboard building. The bell over the door jingled as they stepped inside. Last week, the sweet smell of freshly baked cookies greeted her, but this morning coffee and cinnamon rolls caused her empty stomach to growl.

"Something smells yummy." Henry looked up and grinned.

"Good morning. It's nice to see you two again." Nellie scurried from behind the counter wearing a yellow apron. Smears of flour dotted her face. She gave Caitlyn a hug before turning to Henry. "I've just taken a fresh batch of cinnamon rolls out of the oven. Would you like one?"

Henry turned to Caitlyn. "May I?"

"Of course, you may," Caitlyn answered.

"They just need to sit a minute or two. So, what brings you two out so early? I thought Saturday mornings were for watching cartoons in your jammies and eating sugary cereal." Nellie ruffled the top of Henry's hair.

Caitlyn slipped her grocery list from her crossover bag. "I need to pick up some ingredients to bake a German chocolate cake. It's my mother's recipe," Caitlyn noted.

"Mom likes to bake when she's nervous," Henry added.

Caitlyn shot Henry a look.

"What? That's what Mr. Jeffrey used to say." Henry shrugged his shoulders.

Caitlyn's ex used to say a lot of things in front of Henry that he shouldn't have said. "I'm baking the cake for the Memorial Day cookout tomorrow."

Nellie clapped her hands together. "I'm so happy to hear that you and Henry are planning to attend. You'll have a wonderful time. It's a special day of fellowship to honor the brave individuals who've served our country."

"We are both looking forward to it." Caitlyn caught a whiff of the freshly brewed coffee. "I'd love a cup of that coffee. It smells delicious." Caitlyn inhaled the rich scent and took in her surroundings. Seeing the store aisles her mother had once roamed every Saturday triggered bittersweet memories. The heaviness of the realization settled upon her. She almost couldn't breathe.

Nellie stepped closer and placed her hand on Caitlyn's arm. "Are you okay, dear? You look a little pale."

Caitlyn glanced at Henry, who had wandered over to the enclosed glass cabinet at the back of the store. The shelves housed nostalgic candies, giant jawbreakers, colorful lollipops, and classic candy bars. Her heart squeezed as she watched Henry's eyes fixate on the jawbreakers. He leaned in closer to the cabinet, examining the candies with intense curiosity. It was exactly what she had done many years earlier. Caitlyn swallowed the lump that had formed deep in her throat. "Being here—it's a little overwhelming."

"Let's have a seat." Nellie guided Caitlyn to the corner of the store. Four small round tables were arranged beside a window overlooking a courtyard filled with flowers and trees. "I'll get your coffee. Wait right here." Nellie pulled out the chair. It screeched across the hardwood floor.

Caitlyn sat down and inhaled three deep breaths. What she'd thought was a negative reaction to her surroundings had somehow turned into a calm delight. She felt as though she'd come home. Of course, Bluebell wasn't her home. It had so many bad memories. But for every negative memory, Caitlyn could remember good ones.

Nellie approached the table with a tray. She placed the bone-china cup, hand-painted with yellow daisies, along with a saucer, pitcher of cream, spoon and bowl of sugar in front of Caitlyn. "Here you go, dear."

"Thank you." Caitlyn poured a dash of cream into the cup and stirred. "I was just thinking about my mom."

Nellie slipped into the empty chair. "She was a special lady."

Caitlyn nodded. "I remember my first day of second grade. I'd had a horrible day.

Someone had taken my lunch box from the coat closet and filled it with sand from the playground. The teacher discovered it was a classmate who'd snuck into the room during recess to carry out the prank. His name was Joey Littleton. He had a crush on me and thought that was a way to get my attention. All the kids in my class teased me. My mom brought me here for ice cream. She thought it would make me feel better."

"And did it?" Nellie reached across the table and placed her hand on Caitlyn's wrist.

Caitlyn brushed the tear that raced down her cheek and nodded. "She always made everything better. That afternoon was the last time she was there to comfort me. She and my dad died in the car accident two days later."

"I remember when I first heard. It was such a shock. Your parents were pillars of the community and loved by everyone," Nellie said. "I know you don't plan to stay in town forever, but while you're here, I'd be happy to share stories about them, if you'd like." Nellie squeezed Caitlyn's hand.

"I'd like that." Caitlyn took a sip of her coffee and smiled. A part of her wished she could stay in Bluebell long enough to hear every story Nellie had to tell about her parents, but that wasn't possible. If she lingered, she would get stuck and wouldn't be moving forward toward her dream and what was best for Henry.

Lingering wasn't an option for Caitlyn.

Next to the annual Fourth of July celebration, the Memorial Day picnic held a special place in Logan's heart. It was a time to honor and remember those who had given their lives fighting for the country's freedom, but it also carried a bittersweet memory. Two years ago, after the last fireworks had faded into the darkness, Logan had taken Melody for a walk under the stars. With only the sound of crickets filling the night air, Logan had felt a sense of contentment wash over him when he dropped to one knee and asked Melody to be his wife. Wide-eyed and glowing underneath the full moon, she'd said yes.

Logan neared his brother's house. The farm field to his left was now a makeshift parking lot. Three dozen parked cars flattened the grass, leaving behind tire tracks that looked like a maze. A few members from church still jostled for positions. Logan navigated his vehicle to the front of the residence and parked.

"Uncle Logan! Uncle Logan!"

Logan pulled himself back into the moment and glanced out the window of his truck. He spotted his adorable twin niece and nephew, Kyle and Kayla, running through the field toward the gravel driveway in front of Jake's house.

Their arms pumping them forward as the sound of laughter filled the air. Logan's brother had lost his first wife and their unborn child. God had carried him through the challenging season and blessed him with a loving woman who'd given him a third child, Maddie.

Logan unfastened his seat belt and jumped from the truck. Rocky let out a bark from the back seat. "Hold on, fella. I haven't forgotten you."

"Can we take Rocky for a walk?" Kyle reached the truck first.

Logan attached Rocky's leash to the leather collar. Still kneeling, he turned to the breathless children. "Don't I get a hug first?" Having seen Rocky grow up from a puppy, the twins loved the dog especially.

Kayla was the first to fling her arms around Logan's neck. "Sorry! We're just excited to see Rocky. Miss Myrna brought Callie, too. She said we could take her for a walk once she asks Daddy for permission. We thought we could take both at the same time."

Jake had trained Callie to assist his dear friend, Myrna Hart, following a diagnosis of macular degeneration. "Do you think you can handle both dogs?"

Kayla pulled away from Logan and Kyle stepped up to give his uncle a quick hug. "Sure we can. Kayla can walk Callie, since they're both girls. I'll take Rocky. He's bigger and I'm stronger." Kyle stated his case and squared his slim shoulders.

"That sounds like a plan." Logan passed the leash to Kyle. "You hang on to Rocky while I get the hamburger and hot dog rolls out of the back. Kayla, you can help me."

"Sure, Uncle Logan." Kayla rounded the vehicle.

Logan opened the back of the truck and turned to the sound of tires crunching on loose stones. He peered over his shoulder and smiled when he spotted the familiar SUV. *Caitlyn.* His pulse increased. When he'd extended the invitation the other day, he'd sensed a bit of hesitancy, so he wasn't sure if she'd definitely show up. Logan was positive if she'd had a moment of hesitation, Henry had changed her mind.

"Who's that?" Kayla asked.

"That's a friend of your uncle Luke's, but now she is also our friend. She has a son named Henry who is just about your age. He's a little shy, so let's make him feel welcome," Logan instructed the twins, even though both Kayla and Kyle always treated other children with respect.

"Cool!" Kyle sang out. "Maybe Henry can go for a walk with us."

It hadn't taken Logan long to learn Caitlyn was protective with her son. He didn't want her to feel in an uncomfortable position by having the children ask to whisk her son away. "Why don't we get to know each other first? Then maybe later you can go for that walk."

Logan unloaded the bags of groceries from the truck, along with a tank of propane for Jake's grill. He placed the tank on the ground as Caitlyn rolled up behind him.

"Hi. Should I park over there?" Caitlyn stuck her head out the window of the SUV and pointed toward the parked cars.

Caitlyn's eyes gazed into his, causing warmth to course through him. Maybe she wanted to attend the picnic. "No, you can stay right where you are." Logan motioned with his hand for her to pull up a few feet before he halted. "Perfect." He returned his focus to unpacking his truck.

Moments later the SUV's doors slammed. Logan glanced over his shoulder. When he spotted Caitlyn walking toward him, the warmth he'd felt a couple of minutes earlier suddenly turned into a raging inferno. And it wasn't the late May sun beating down on his face, creating this reaction. It was all Caitlyn. Wow! She wore a floral, cotton sundress that billowed in the gentle breeze, paired with pink, strappy sandals. Her hair flowed loosely over her shoulders. She looked incredible. Logan used his left hand to steady himself against the truck as she approached.

Caitlyn's attire differed from what Logan had spotted her wearing in church only hours earlier. Five minutes into the service, wearing black slacks and a light blue blouse, Caitlyn and Henry had slipped into the back row. Henry had dropped a hymnal that had prompted Logan to turn toward the rear of the church. For a second, Caitlyn and Logan's eyes had connected before she'd picked up the hymnal and sang along with the congregation. He had hoped to catch up with her after worship. Instead of going to the fellowship hall with Henry, Caitlyn had scampered out of the building like a sandpiper.

"Hi, Mr. Logan!" Henry was the first to speak while Logan tried to get his tongue unraveled.

"Hi!" The twins stepped up and greeted the twosome.

Logan's mouth felt like he had ten large cotton balls stuffed inside as he took tentative steps toward Caitlyn. His eyes locked on her demure smile. She looked nothing like the woman who furrowed her brow while poring over her journal filled with endless lists and thoughts.

As he drew closer, Logan could not keep his reaction to her presence to himself. "You look beautiful," he finally breathed, his voice barely a whisper. Caitlyn's cheeks ignited with a rosy blush and he couldn't help but feel a twinge of doubt. Was he wrong to admit to the effect she had on him? Right or wrong, he spoke the truth.

"Thank you." Caitlyn glanced down at her outfit. "I hope

I'm dressed appropriately." She tucked a strand of hair behind her ear.

"I told her she should wear jeans in case there's a potato sack race or something," Henry stated.

Logan ruffled the top of Henry's head. "Your mom made the right choice."

"She sure took long enough to decide. I thought we'd never get out of the house." Henry rolled his eyes.

Logan faked a cough to hide the humor he found in Henry's words. "How are you doing today, buddy? Are you ready to have some fun?"

"I sure am! We don't get to do stuff like this much at home. Mom is always so busy with her school and worrying about stuff," Henry lamented.

Logan noticed Caitlyn's earlier expression had faded. "Well, I can guarantee both of you will have a great time today." Logan turned to the twins and Rocky. "First, I want you to meet my niece and nephew. This is Kayla and Kyle." Logan placed a hand on each child. "They'll both make sure you enjoy yourselves today. Of course, you already know Rocky."

"It's nice to meet you." Caitlyn smiled.

"Hi," Henry chirped and knelt to the ground in front of Rocky. "Hey, Rocky—remember me?"

Rocky's tail wagged with rapid, frenzied movements. Without hesitation, the dog jumped to greet Henry, smothering his face with sloppy kisses. As Rocky continued to shower Henry with affection, Henry giggled and rolled over on his back, finally giving in to the dog's relentless attention.

Kyle dropped to the ground alongside Henry to join in the fun. "Rocky really likes you."

"You think so?" Henry wiped away the dog drool from his cheek.

Kayla joined the boys. "Yeah, he doesn't act like this with just anyone."

Logan turned his attention from the children to Caitlyn. Not that his awareness had faded since she'd stepped out of her truck. "Did you enjoy Pastor Kidd's sermon this morning?" The message on worry couldn't have come at a more perfect time. Since Caitlyn's arrival, Logan worried he'd lose the land along with his dream of creating the dog rescue organization. The pastor's words reminded him not to be anxious and to continue to let his requests be known to God. In the end, it would all work out. Of course, some days not allowing his mind to follow the worry trail was easier said than done.

Caitlyn nodded. "I did. He even captured Henry's attention. He kept nudging me. And on the way home, he reminded me I was wasting too much time worrying." Caitlyn touched her throat. "Sometimes it's hard for me to believe he's only seven years old."

Logan glanced at Henry, chatting with Kayla and Kyle as though they were lifelong friends. "Yeah, I've learned a lot from those two." Logan tipped his head toward the twins before he turned his attention back to Caitlyn. "I tried to catch up with you after the service. I wanted to grab a cup of coffee with you in the fellowship hall, but you ran out like the church was on fire," Logan joked.

Caitlyn dug the toe of her sandal into the gravel. "I wanted to have plenty of time to run back to Luke's house to change and pick up the cake that I baked."

"I'm glad I didn't catch up to you then. You really look great."

"It's been a while since I've worn a dress. Back home, jeans and T-shirts are my go-to attire," Caitlyn said.

Logan watched as Caitlyn fingered the silver necklace with a hummingbird pendant. "Well, no matter what you wear, I'm sure the guys in your town would walk on hot rocks for a date with you." Logan waited for Caitlyn's response and it was worth the wait. Her eyes sparkled and a playful smile danced across her lips. In the time they'd spent together, he'd never heard her mention a husband or boyfriend. There was a part of him that wanted to know so much more about Caitlyn, but he didn't want to scare her away. Perhaps today would be the day she might open up and reveal a secret or two.

Chapter Eight

Somewhere along the line, Caitlyn's plan to keep her focus on revitalizing the farmhouse and off of Logan had flopped like a cake removed from the oven too soon. Something stirred inside and had come alive when he'd told her she looked beautiful. Caitlyn couldn't remember the last time a man spoke those words to her. Was that why she was reacting this way, because no man had paid her a compliment in forever? Or could it be because Logan was the one who'd paid the compliment, and he was the most gorgeous man she'd ever known?

"Thanks for carrying the grocery bags for me," Logan called out over his shoulder. "Don't worry about Henry. The kids will be fine walking the dogs. Kayla has already developed that motherly instinct. She's great with her baby sister, Maddie."

Caitlyn had had reservations when Kyle had suggested Henry join him and Kayla while they walked Rocky and the other dog, Callie. But when she'd noticed the excitement in Henry's eyes, she couldn't say no. He longed to do things on his own, like other children.

Caitlyn trekked across the well-manicured lawn to the patio with the cake carrier in her hands and two bags hanging from each wrist. Logan led the way, carrying the propane. He placed the tank on the oversize patio.

"Wow, that's an impressive outdoor kitchen." The stainless-steel cabinets next to the six-burner grill gleamed in the sunlight.

"Yeah. Jake built it for the family to enjoy. In March, when Pastor Kidd announced the town was in search of a venue for the Memorial Day picnic this year, Jake was the first to raise his hand. Let me introduce you to him." Logan placed the backup propane tank off to the side of the patio.

Caitlyn's heart raced with anticipation as she realized she was about to meet Logan's older brother. She already knew Luke, Logan's younger brother, so why did she feel nervous now? She bit her lip to calm her nerves.

"There he is." Logan pointed.

Jake stood over the grill, flipping burgers with a practiced ease. From behind, he appeared tall and muscular, dressed in jeans, a white shirt, along with a brown cowboy hat.

"Hey, buddy," Logan called.

Jake turned and displayed the same chiseled features as an older version of Logan. Salt-and-pepper hair peeked out from underneath the hat. He looked over and threw off a wave, the spatula in his hand, as they approached.

"Hey there." Jake placed the utensil on the side table and extended his hand. "You must be Caitlyn. I'm happy you came today. Logan's told me all about you and the farmhouse renovations."

Caitlyn's cheeks flushed under his intense gaze as she greeted Jake. His grip was firm. "I've heard a lot about you as well. I made a German chocolate cake." She handed off the dessert.

"That's a favorite around here. Thank you very much." Jake placed the cake on the table behind him.

"Thank you for welcoming me and my son to your beautiful home." Caitlyn smiled.

"Any friend of Logan and Luke's is a friend of mine." Jake scanned the area. "I wanted to introduce you to my wife, Olivia, but she must be inside with Nellie getting the side dishes together."

"Hosting a large function like this is a lot of work. I'll look forward to meeting your wife later when she's not busy. Your children are delightful. We met earlier. You should be proud," Caitlyn said.

Jake tipped the brim of his hat. "Thank you. I could say the same to you. I had a brief introduction to Henry before he headed off with the kids to walk the dogs."

"Thanks, I appreciate the twin's hospitality. Henry can be a little shy," Caitlyn explained.

Logan patted his brother on the shoulder. "We better let you get back to work. Looks like a sizeable crowd, which means a lot of hungry mouths to feed."

Caitlyn's attention turned to the growing commotion near the beverage table. A line snaked around the table like a ribbon. Laughter filled the air as more guests gathered, shaking hands and welcoming one another. Caitlyn couldn't think of any place she'd rather be. "Would you like for me to help you serve?" she offered.

Jake shook his head. "No way. I appreciate the offer, but I want you and my brother to relax and enjoy the day. He doesn't slow down too often, so I'm hoping you can show him how." Jake winked.

"Thanks, buddy. I'll try. But you know me," Logan drawled.

"Why don't you grab some food and take Caitlyn up on

the swing? I've placed a couple of tables up there." Jake glanced at the few fluffy clouds drifting lazily across the vibrant blue expanse. "With a sky like this, the view should be nothing short of spectacular."

Logan tipped his chin. "I was thinking the same thing." He turned to Caitlyn. "Let's eat."

A few minutes later, Caitlyn spotted the oversize swing underneath the towering Douglas fir tree. She splayed her fingers across her chest. "This view is absolutely breathtaking. I don't think I've ever seen the Rocky Mountains this clearly."

As she and Logan approached, the tree's sheer size left her in awe. The thick trunk and sprawling branches seemed to reach endlessly toward the sky. Suspended by sturdy chains, the swing creaked in the gentle breeze that rustled through the trees.

Caitlyn couldn't resist. She plopped down on the wooden bench and extended her legs out in front, kicking her feet like an excited child. "I could stay here forever." She inhaled a deep breath of the crisp mountain air.

Logan laughed as he took a seat next to Caitlyn. "That's exactly what my sister-in-law said the first time Jake brought her here."

"Really?" Caitlyn rested her head on the plank.

"She sure did." Logan stood, holding both plates of food. "We could eat our burgers here, if you'd like."

"That sounds perfect." Caitlyn accepted her plate as Logan settled in.

"Yeah, when Jake tells the story, he likes to say this swing is the reason Olivia made Bluebell her permanent home. She worked as an ER doctor in Miami." Logan laughed and started a forward motion of the swing.

The wood squeaked softly beneath them as they ate their

burgers and munched on potato salad. An aroma mixed with sweet onions and meat drifted from the patio. Sounds of children laughing and adults chattering filled the air.

"Actually, this is where he proposed to Olivia."

Caitlyn closed her eyes for a second and tried to picture the scene. She couldn't think of a more romantic place to ask someone to spend the rest of their lives together. It was something she'd dreamed of, but as the years slipped away, and after the breakup, Caitlyn accepted the fact that it would be her and Henry. "I can't imagine any woman saying no to a proposal made here. This is like a setting for a romance novel."

"I'll make a note of that," Logan responded before tasting his burger.

"So you've never brought a girl up here to propose?" Caitlyn joked.

Logan swallowed. "Not here." He took another bite.

Wait. Logan wasn't married. Did that mean he was engaged? If so, why hadn't he mentioned a fiancée? Where was she? Or maybe, like she and Jeffrey, they'd parted ways.

"I can hear the questions rolling around in your head," Logan quipped.

Busted. She was breaking her own rule. No exchanging of personal information. By keeping things all business, there would be no emotional attachment. Well, maybe this one time wouldn't hurt.

"So, are you engaged to be married?" Caitlyn nibbled on her burger and peered at Logan from the corner of her eyes.

"I was. In fact, Lester and his wife introduced me to Melody. Thelma had known her since she was a little girl."

Maybe Melody had dumped Logan like Jeffrey had ditched her? Was that even possible? The woman would have to be an egg short of a dozen to break up with Logan. From what she'd seen, he was exactly like his brother Jake—sweet, kind, great with children, and gorgeous.

"Melody died over a year ago," Logan stated and stared straight ahead.

Caitlyn gasped and covered her mouth with her hand. "I'm so sorry." Thoughts swirled in her head. How? Why? But Logan said nothing more. They continued to eat their meal in silence while swinging and looking out onto the sweeping mountains stretching across the horizon.

Logan wasn't about to allow his past mistake to ruin Caitlyn's day at the picnic. Today was her first day off since arriving in Bluebell and working nonstop on the farmhouse. The second he'd mentioned Melody, regret numbed his mind. Pain and shock reflected in her eyes. Logan wanted to keep the mood more lighthearted, but he had opened the door to his past. He prepared himself to answer Caitlyn's questions, but for the past ten minutes, she had remained quiet.

"A couple months before the wedding, Melody and I had an appointment in Denver to meet with the wedding photographer." Logan remembered how he'd felt that morning. He'd woken up the day of the appointment drenched in sweat. Then a sudden chill had run through him, causing him to convulse. His body had felt heavy and nonresponsive until a deep hacking cough had erupted in his chest, igniting waves of pain through every bone and muscle in his body. "That morning, I woke up with the worst case of the flu I'd ever had."

Caitlyn remained silent.

Logan inhaled a deep breath and continued. "When I phoned Melody to tell her I was sick, she wanted to reschedule the appointment. I knew how important getting the right photographer was to her, so I insisted she take my new Range Rover to the city to meet with the photographer without me. Her car was older, and it had been in and out of the garage for repairs. I thought my vehicle would be safer. I was wrong." Logan looked up toward the sky and prayed silently for the strength to continue recalling the worst day of his life.

"You don't have to say any more. I know how difficult it can be to talk about a car accident that takes away a loved one," Caitlyn said.

Of course, after losing her parents in a car accident, Caitlyn would assume that was how Melody had lost her life. Especially based on what he'd told her so far. Logan shook his head. "No, Pastor Kidd told me I should talk about it. The thing is Melody didn't die in a car accident. She died because of me. I wasn't there when some guy with a gun approached her in the parking garage and wanted my fancy new car. If I'd let Melody take her beat-up clunker, she'd still be alive."

Caitlyn gasped. She reached out and placed her hand on Logan's arm. "Oh, Logan, I didn't know. I'm so sorry."

Logan shook his head. His eyes brimmed with tears. "When I got the call from a Denver state trooper, I thought I was delirious from the fever. At first, I didn't believe him. I wanted it to be a bad dream. But when I had to call her parents, it all became real. Telling her mom and dad that they'd lost their baby girl was the hardest thing I've ever had to do."

Caitlyn moved her hand slowly up and down Logan's arm.

"You're a good listener. Thank you." Logan's brothers

were constantly telling him to get past it, to move on. Not that easy when it should have been him.

"I'm here whenever you want to talk. It's not good to keep things bottled up inside," Caitlyn said.

"I appreciate that." Logan didn't see a need to go into the worst details of the dreadful day. "I hadn't planned on unloading all of this on you, today especially." Caitlyn's touch provided comfort, but it didn't stop the guilt that he carried daily. He just had to keep putting one foot in front of the other and trust that God would one day heal his wounds. But today wasn't about wallowing in his grief.

Logan straightened his shoulders. "What I'd really had in mind when I brought you to this special place was to learn more about you."

"Oh, really?" Caitlyn grinned.

"So—are you seeing anyone?"

Caitlyn jerked her head in Logan's direction.

Logan laughed and Caitlyn joined in.

"You don't beat around the bush, Mr. Beckett." Caitlyn chuckled, shooting him a sly look before turning her attention back to the view.

"We have been spending a lot of time together. It's only natural for me to wonder if there is someone waiting for you back home in Wyoming." Logan couldn't imagine Caitlyn didn't have men lining up to date her. She was charming and beautiful, plus she had a quick wit, something he always found attractive in a woman.

"Let's see, the guy who runs the local tack and supply shop is always waiting for me to come in with my horses to have them re-shoed." Caitlyn twirled a strand of her hair around her finger.

"And?" Logan leaned in and noticed her familiar honeysuckle-scented shampoo.

"He replaces the shoes for my horses and then I go home," Caitlyn answered.

"So you're not dating him?"

Caitlyn giggled. "He's nearing eighty years old and has been married since he was sixteen."

Logan's eyes danced in amusement and a small smile parted his lips. The playful banter was a welcome reprieve from the seriousness of the previous conversation. "Let's forget that guy. Is there anyone else in the picture?"

Caitlyn's smile faded and her shoulders dropped. "There was someone a while ago—but it's over now."

Logan waited for Caitlyn to expand a little on the relationship that had ended, but she remained quiet, examining her fingernails. "I'm sorry. I shouldn't be prying into your personal life. Just because I spilled my guts doesn't mean you have to do the same."

"There's no need to apologize. In hindsight, the breakup was probably for the best. Jeffrey, that's his name, and I wanted different things." She leaned back against the swing.

"Relationships can be hard enough without having common goals. How did Henry take it when things ended?" Logan wanted to know more, but he didn't want to push Caitlyn. Then again, when would they have time alone like this? "Did he like the guy?"

"When Jeffrey and I first started dating, I was already fostering Henry. I kept those two parts of my life separate, but I made sure Jeffrey was aware of my plan to one day adopt Henry. Once the adoption process was complete, the three of us spent more time together. Jeffrey was good to Henry. He liked to buy him things and take him to fun places, but there was never an emotional connection between the two of them. Henry is an intuitive little boy. I think he sensed Jeffrey preferred when he wasn't around." Caitlyn picked at the hem of her sundress.

"I didn't mean to upset you." Logan shifted closer to her. It had to have been difficult for Caitlyn to keep two parts of her life separate and then gradually join them together.

Caitlyn rolled her shoulders. "No, you didn't. I should have ended things before he did. In fairness to Jeffrey, circumstances in my life changed dramatically after the adoption, so I can't put all the blame on him."

Logan admired Caitlyn. When relationships fail, it's easy to put the fault on the other person. "Well, Jeffrey is missing out. Henry is a great kid."

Caitlyn rested her head against the swing and glanced up to the sky. "I can't imagine my life without him."

Enjoying the sounds of nature and the gentle motion of the swing, Logan wasn't quite ready for his alone time with Caitlyn to end. A part of him wanted to stay and watch the sunset with her, but Logan knew they couldn't ignore the fact that there was a community picnic happening. "Do you think we'd better head back and be social?" Logan asked.

A low rumble sounded in the distance.

"What was that?" Caitlyn turned to Logan.

"Maybe it was someone's truck."

"Look!" Caitlyn pointed to the dark clouds gathering on the horizon, their edges illuminated by the last rays of the sun. "I think a storm is coming."

Logan looked up and spotted ominous clouds, lightning flickering inside, moving in their direction. Gusts of wind whipped through the trees. Logan sprang from the swing and grabbed Caitlyn's hand. "We need to get back to the house as fast as we can." Running across the open field during an electrical storm was too dangerous. They had to outrun the storm clouds and take shelter before the storm hit.

"Henry!" Caitlyn cried out.

"He's probably back at the house. We need to hurry." Logan shot glances at the clouds.

"I can't run in these sandals." Caitlyn shouted as she bent over and stripped the shoes from her feet.

"Hold my hand and run as fast as you can," Logan instructed her.

Splat. A fat raindrop hit Logan's cheek, followed by another. Seconds later, the storm clouds above opened, stinging their bodies like a swarm of bees, soaking their clothes. The ground beneath their feet shook as the thunder grew louder. It was too late. The storm was right over top of them. Logan and Caitlyn were in the most dangerous place to be—a wide-open field.

Chapter Nine

"Get inside, quick!" Logan called out when they finally reached Jake's house.

Caitlyn's bare feet skidded across the slick stone as she felt Logan's hand strong against her back, guiding her through the open patio door. Safe from the elements, but not knowing whether Henry was still outside with the dogs, she scanned the family room area. People packed Jake's house, seeking shelter from the storm. Her eyes ran over the area a second time. There was no sign of him. Her heart pounded in her chest. "I have to find Henry!" she cried out to no one in particular. Her voice filled with worry.

Logan stepped closer. "He could be inside. There's Olivia." Logan pointed to the tall, slender woman speaking with Nellie. "Olivia!" Logan motioned her over.

Caitlyn couldn't stand still so she met the woman halfway. "Have you seen my son? He's with your children."

Olivia placed her hand on Caitlyn's arm. "Jake went out to look for the kids. Don't worry. He'll be back with them any minute."

Caitlyn's heart sank. Her worst fear had come true. The entire time she'd raced through the open field, running from the storm, she had prayed that Henry and the twins were safe in the house. She should have never allowed him to go off for a walk without adult supervision. How could she be so irresponsible?

"Kayla!" Logan shouted.

Caitlyn turned to the open patio door and spotted Kayla. Her hair was soaking wet. The denim shorts she wore dripped water like a faucet onto the hardwood floor.

Caitlyn sprinted toward Kayla. She dropped to her knees in front of the child and placed her hands on her forearms. "Where are Henry and Kyle?" she asked, foregoing her inside voice.

"I don't know," Kayla cried.

The piercing sound of cell phones blaring storm warnings filled the room.

Caitlyn's heart raced.

Olivia joined her daughter's side. "Sweetie, where did you last see them?"

Kayla's lip quivered. "Henry wanted to walk on the trail at the pond, so he could visit Donald, the duck. We kept telling him we shouldn't go that far, but he said he had to see him."

The hollow pit in Caitlyn's stomach widened. Henry didn't know how to swim.

Nellie approached the group with a large bath towel and draped it over Kayla's head like a wedding veil. "Here, sweetie, try to dry off a little."

"Thank you, Nellie." Olivia used the end of the towel to dry Kayla's face.

"Did you make it to the water?" Logan asked before taking a quick glance at Caitlyn.

Caitlyn used her hand to cover her mouth. The look in Logan's eyes told her he remembered Henry didn't know how to swim. Swimming lessons. It was on her list of things to do.

Kayla nodded. "When we got closer to the pond, Kyle

let Callie off her leash so she could run down to the water. I told him not to, but he didn't listen. Then we heard the thunder, and it started raining. Kyle couldn't get Callie back on the leash. I think the storm scared her because she took off running toward Uncle Logan's house. I came back here as quick as I could. Are they going to be okay?" Kayla looked up at the adults with tears streaming down her face.

Caitlyn heard the rain pounding against the roof. The muscles in her legs tightened, readying herself to run out the door. She turned to Logan. "How do I get to the pond from here?"

"No, the storm is right over us. I can't—" Logan hesitated for a second and drew in a breath "—I won't let you go. It's too dangerous out there. We need to wait for the storm to pass."

Allowing Henry to go off with Kyle and Kayla had been a big mistake. Caitlyn knew better than that. She was his mother—his protector. Under normal circumstances, she would have never allowed this. She'd let down her guard. For what? Time alone with Logan? Was that the reason Caitlyn had given Henry permission? Her mind reeled with possibilities. What if his anxiety from the storm triggered a seizure? Who will help him? "My son is out there. I can't leave him alone. He doesn't know the property. He'll never be able to find his way back."

Olivia stepped closer to Caitlyn. "I know we've never met and I hate that it's happening under these dreadful circumstances, but I want to reassure you that Kyle knows every inch of this property. We've taught him what to do if he's caught in any type of inclement weather, particularly thunderstorms. Please wait here. It won't do anyone any good if you go out in the middle of the storm and get hurt."

Caitlyn felt an instant bond with Olivia. She knew Jake's

wife was right, but how could she just stand there and do nothing?

Caitlyn walked to the window, but the blinding rain didn't allow her to see beyond the glass. A few seconds ticked by before little balls of ice pecked against the window. "It's hailing!" Suddenly, tiny pellets grew to the size of golf balls and knocked against the glass. A memory flashed in her mind from last summer. While transporting a new horse from Montana back to Wyoming, Caitlyn had gotten caught in a horrible hail storm. Thankfully, she'd made it to an underpass where she'd rode out the storm that had produced hailstones the size of softballs. Caitlyn had witnessed the aftermath. Dented cars and trucks littered the highway with front and rear windshields shattered, the roofs smashed like tin cans. Glass and other debris had cluttered the asphalt. Caitlyn had spent the entire ride home thanking God for providing a refuge from the fierce storm.

"Everyone move away from the windows and skylights!" Logan instructed the crowd.

Overhead, the roof sounded as though it were being pummeled with rocks.

Caitlyn's knees felt locked as she forced herself to step back from the glass. She noticed Logan and Olivia exchanging glances. Their concern was palpable. "We can't just stand here! Our children are in danger!" Caitlyn directed her words toward Olivia. She hoped another mother would understand the hopelessness she felt. But Olivia only moved away from the window with no sign that she planned to head outside and look for the children.

Moments later, as suddenly as the hail arrived, it departed as though someone had turned off a switch. The banging on the roof subsided, replaced by the sound of heavy rain.

Caitlyn rubbed the back of her neck and turned to Logan. "Since the hail has passed, can we at least get in your truck and drive to your house? Kayla mentioned they went in that direction." If Logan said no, Caitlyn was ready to jump in her own SUV to look for Henry.

Logan nodded. "We can."

Caitlyn pressed her hand to her stomach and released a sigh of relief.

"I need to call Jake with an update. Let me check the weather app to make sure the worst of the storm has cleared before we venture outdoors."

"Jake was in such a hurry, he ran off without his phone. It's still in the kitchen," Olivia said.

Logan pulled his phone from his pocket, swiped and tapped. "The storm is moving east, so we should be okay." He returned the device to its original spot. "I'll pull my truck around front. If you'd like, you can wait for me on the porch," Logan instructed Caitlyn before he jogged out the door.

"I'll get you a pair of tennis shoes. You can't be traipsing outside in your bare feet with all the mud and debris on the ground. Can you wear a size eight?" Olivia asked.

"That's exactly my size." She watched Olivia move swiftly out of the room. Caitlyn rubbed her hands up and down her arms to warm the sudden chill.

As quickly as Olivia left the room, she returned carrying a pair of neon-green tennis shoes. "Logan won't lose sight of you in these." She laughed and handed the shoes to Caitlyn.

"I have the same color at home." Caitlyn examined the footwear. Under different circumstances, Caitlyn and Olivia could be good friends.

"I brought you a sweater, too. Following a hailstorm, the temperature drops," Olivia explained.

"That's very kind of you. Thank you."

"Don't worry, Miss Caitlyn. My brother Kyle will take care of Henry. He's really good with outdoor stuff. He's a Cub Scout."

Caitlyn looked down at the drenched girl and smiled. "Thank you, sweetie."

"Here's the sweater." Olivia moved closer and placed the pale yellow cardigan over Caitlyn's shoulders.

Logan's horn honked out front.

"Thank you." Caitlyn slipped on the garment and headed out the door.

Olivia was right about the weather. The sweater did little to protect Caitlyn from the arctic blast of air. A chill ran through her body the second she stepped outside. The temperature must have dropped over twenty degrees. She noticed the blue flax that had once lined the sidewalk leading to the front porch was flat on the ground from the hailstones.

Logan jumped from the truck and rounded the vehicle. Rain splattered against Caitlyn's face as he opened the door and she climbed inside. She didn't see any hail damage on Logan's truck, but sometimes it was more visible depending on how the sun hit the vehicle. Caitlyn gazed up at Jake's roof, looking for any visible damage. Thoughts of the new roof on her farmhouse entered her mind. Had it remained unscathed? Right now, that was the least of her worries. Finding Henry safe was her top priority.

Logan buckled his seat belt and jammed his foot down on the accelerator. The rear wheels of the truck spun, kicking up clumps of mud and gravel.

Caitlyn remained quiet, staring straight ahead while smoothing her sundress.

"My brothers and I have talked about paving a road to

connect our properties. But the estimates we've received from asphalt companies in Denver were outrageous." Logan hoped to squash the silence inside the cab. Caitlyn blamed herself for Henry getting lost in the storm. Logan understood the burden of carrying guilt.

Several minutes later, Logan released a sigh of relief when they arrived at his house. The storm had passed and the late-afternoon sun filtered through the cirrus clouds drifting overhead. He navigated the truck up the gravel driveway and parked in front of the home.

Caitlyn didn't wait for Logan to come around and open up her door. She flew out of the vehicle before he turned off the ignition. She scanned the property with her hands on her hips. "Where should we look?"

"Kyle knows where I hide the spare key. If the boys made it this far, they would have gotten inside the house with no problem. Let's go see." Logan motioned for her to follow.

They ran up the four brick steps leading to the front porch. Outside the door, Logan fumbled for the house key in his pocket. He slipped it into the lock and turned the knob. "Kyle! Henry! Are you in here?" Logan's shoulders dropped. They hadn't been able to seek shelter in his house.

"What do we do now?" Caitlyn's voice echoed in the foyer.

"Kayla mentioned Henry wanted to see Donald. We can start here and follow the trail to the pond. We've walked the path so many times, Kyle could probably find his way blindfolded."

Caitlyn squeezed her eyes shut and then opened them. "After that violent storm, I can't imagine they would still be down there—unless they're both hurt," she whimpered.

Logan reached for Caitlyn's arm. "You've got to trust me. I know Kyle. He wouldn't stay out in the weather we just experienced. I've taught him to respect the power of Mother Nature. My thought is since the storm has passed, the boys might have headed back to the pond to make sure Donald is safe."

Caitlyn's shoulders relaxed slightly. "You're right. That's exactly what Henry would want to do."

"Let's get going," Logan said.

Minutes later, Logan and Caitlyn dashed along the muddy trail. Thunder rumbled faintly in the distance. Logan's heart pounded with adrenaline. The aftermath of the thunderstorm left behind rain-soaked grass and broken tree branches. Thanks to the tennis shoes Olivia had loaned Caitlyn, she could maneuver the slippery terrain. Both were undeterred by the slick conditions.

"How far are we from the pond?" Caitlyn asked over his shoulder. Her feet splashed through the muddy puddles.

"Not far." Logan didn't want to give Caitlyn false hope, but over the next hill was a shed he'd built for his equipment. It was the closest structure to the pond. It would be the most logical spot Kyle would have taken Henry to ride out the storm.

As the two crested the hill, Caitlyn spotted the building. "What's that over there?" She pointed to the newly renovated wooden structure.

"It's one of my sheds. I built it a couple of years ago to store my equipment. I have a feeling that's where Kyle might have gone."

Before Logan finished the sentence, Caitlyn sprinted off at top speed. Her feet slipped and skidded on the muddy trail, causing her to nearly lose her balance a few times. Her legs pumped faster, propelling her forward as she neared the shed.

"Oh, no," Caitlyn shouted from the opposite side of the shed.

Logan rounded the corner to the front of the building. His heart sank when he spotted a large tree that had fallen in front of the double doors, blocking any access to the structure.

"Henry!" Caitlyn pounded on the side wall and gave it a couple of kicks.

"Mom! The door is stuck," Henry yelled.

Logan sent up a silent prayer, giving thanks the boys were safe. Now he had to get the tree out of the way. It was too large for him and Caitlyn to move.

"What about that window?" Caitlyn pointed to the left side of the shed.

Logan considered Caitlyn's suggestion. It would take time to get his tractor down here to pull the tree away from the door—maybe the window was the best option.

"Kyle, can you hear me?" Logan yelled. "Are you boys okay? Is anyone hurt?"

"No, we're fine, but we can't get out," he answered.

"A tree fell in front of the door. It's too big for us to move. Do you see the stepladder against the back wall?" Logan asked.

A few seconds passed. "Yeah, I see it."

"Do you think you and Henry can carry it to the window?" Logan prompted.

"Yeah, we can do it." Kyle spoke with confidence.

Caitlyn grabbed Logan's arm. "I don't know if I want Henry climbing the ladder. That's too dangerous."

"It's not much different from climbing a tree. We can bring Henry out first so Kyle can spot him from below. He'll be fine. It's not that high." Logan attempted to reassure Caitlyn. The look on her face told him he was wasting his breath.

Caitlyn weighed the options. She shot a look at the enormous tree and then back to the window and paused. "Okay, I guess that's the fastest way to get the boys out."

"It will be okay." Logan patted her arm.

After a few minutes, the boys had set the ladder up below the window. Logan was confident they wouldn't have a problem climbing to safety.

"Don't worry, Miss Caitlyn. Henry can reach the window without getting on the top step, but I'll break his fall if anything happens."

Kyle was a perceptive boy. He knew how worried Caitlyn was about Henry.

Logan stole a glance at Caitlyn. "He'll be fine." In less than five minutes, both boys had shimmied through the window. They were safely outside in front of the shed and eager to tell the adults about their big adventure.

From the moment Henry hit the ground, Caitlyn didn't want to let go.

"Mom, you're smothering me." Henry wiggled himself out of Caitlyn's arms. "I'm fine. I had the best time ever with Kyle! He knew just where to go. We ran through pouring rain and made it inside the shed just before big ice balls started bouncing on the roof. It was so cool!"

Logan held his chin high. Thanks to Kyle's quick thinking, the boys weren't seriously injured. He looked down at his nephew and nodded. "I'm proud of you."

Caitlyn moved closer to Kyle and wrapped her arms around him. "Thank you for taking care of Henry."

"You're welcome. I kept a close eye on him." Kyle looked up at Logan. "I'm sorry I let Callie off her leash. She got scared by the thunder and took off. Rocky ran after her. I tried to hold on to the leash, but he was too strong."

"The dogs! I was so worried about the boys, I forgot about them." Caitlyn turned to Logan.

"Don't worry. They run loose around this property all the time, so they know their way around. They'll find their way back home. I'm just glad these two fellas are okay." Logan ruffled the heads of each boy before turning his attention back to Kyle. "Let's get you home. Your mom's probably worrying herself sick."

"What about Donald?" Henry tugged on Logan's arm. "We need to make sure she didn't get hurt in the storm."

Logan tossed a quick glance at Caitlyn.

She nodded at Henry and then said to Kyle, "We can go down to the pond, but first your uncle needs to call your mother and let her know you're okay."

Five minutes later, Logan had shared the good news with Olivia. Jake had showed up at the house, so everyone was safe and accounted for.

Logan guided the group down the path to the pond. The closer they got to the water, the squawks of Canadian geese echoed in the air. "It sounds like the geese weathered the storm," Logan teased.

"I hope Donald is okay." Henry moved purposely ahead.

"I'm sure this isn't the first storm Donald has experienced, and it won't be her last. Animals have good instincts. They know how to protect themselves in bad weather. She's probably swimming around now, trying to get away from the pestering geese." Logan hoped that was the case. It would crush Henry if anything had happened to Donald.

The foursome crested the last hill overlooking the water. Henry ran, pumping his arms. He nearly stumbled several times. Kyle followed his friend.

"Wait! Don't get near the water!" Caitlyn shouted, but Henry ignored his mother's command.

Logan performed a quick assessment around the pond. Several trees a diligent beaver had been working on for the past few months had toppled over from the strong winds. The beaver would have plenty of timber to continue construction of the condo he was attempting to build from one edge of the pond to the other. For the past year, he'd worked hard to build his damn inside the pond. He exemplified the saying busy as a beaver.

Caitlyn and Logan caught up to the boys, who stood on the bank looking for Donald.

"I don't see her anywhere. Do you think the storm blew her away?" Henry kept his eyes focused on the water.

Logan moved closer to Henry. "My guess is Donald took shelter in a tree. She's got good eyes. If we hang out here for a minute, she might see us and come looking for some food."

In the distance, Rocky's familiar bark echoed across the property. Logan turned his back to the water, placed his thumb and his index finger between his lips, and whistled. "Rocky! Come here, boy!"

Seconds later, the barking got louder when Callie joined Rocky.

Caitlyn turned and pointed to the ridge. "Look! Here they come!"

Rocky led the way, with Callie not far behind.

Logan watched as the animals plowed through the overgrown grass and fallen branches, soaked by the rain. Both needed a bath. With their tongues lolling and tails wagging, they appeared happy as ever.

Kyle and Henry broke out in smiles while Caitlyn stood nearby.

"Come here, girl!" Kyle called for Callie, but the dog had other plans.

The group watched as Callie splashed into the water. Rocky followed her lead.

"I guess I don't have to worry about giving them a bath now." Logan crossed his arms over his chest and laughed.

Caitlyn moved toward Henry and knelt in front of him. Obviously relieved to find Henry safe, now she tried to comfort him as he worried about Donald. What was the connection that Henry had with that duck?

Logan stepped closer, hoping to put Henry's mind at ease.

Henry looked up and squinted into the bright sun. "Where do you think Donald could have gone? The wind was so strong. What if she's somewhere in the woods hurt? We need to go look for her." He slowly walked away, his head down, and kicking his tennis shoe into the mud.

Caitlyn turned to Logan. "I've got to let him look for Donald, otherwise I know he'll worry that he didn't do enough to find her."

Logan nodded. "I agree. We can check the wooded area that surrounds the pond. Let's get the dogs."

After an exhaustive hour of combing every nook and cranny around the pond, it was time to call it quits for the day. Henry had remained silent during the entire search.

Logan stopped and gently touched Henry's arm before squatting in front of him. "I know you're worried about Donald. There's a chance the storm scared her so much she's afraid to come back while there's people around the pond. We should head back to my brother's house and give her a chance to come back on her own."

"Okay," Henry responded as the group retreated and headed to Jake's house.

Chapter Ten

Wiring issue.

Check.

Early the following Saturday morning, Caitlyn sat hunched at Luke's kitchen table with her nose buried between the pages of her journal. Her shoulders relaxed. She could finally check off the wiring inspection.

Caitlyn picked up her coffee cup. Its contents sloshed over the rim, leaving two brown stains on the paper. That was the least of her worries.

As she scanned the remaining items on the to-do list, she dropped the pen and placed her fingertips against her temples. Worry had consumed her since three o'clock in the morning. Last weekend's hailstorm had caused damage to many residences in Bluebell while sparing others. Unfortunately, Last Dollar hadn't escaped the wrath of Mother Nature. It might take time, but Logan assured her there was no need to worry. The men who'd initially worked to replace her roof were busy helping the neighbors whose homes had a lot more damage than her farmhouse.

Besides the repairs, Henry had worried himself sick over Donald. Since the storm, the duck was still missing. With each day that passed, Henry complained more and more about an upset stomach. Caitlyn had done her best to keep his mind off Donald, but it was a losing battle.

Fortunately, the past week had delivered some good news. Lester returned and had worked on the wiring. Now everything was up to code.

Focus on the good. That was her mantra. Lately, the early morning hours were the time of day when Caitlyn had to guard her thoughts, especially with her financial situation. It was easy to become overwhelmed by the projects that still had to be addressed. She needed to keep her focus on the progress made with the help of the good people of Bluebell.

"Can we look for Donald today?" Henry entered the kitchen, rubbing his eyes. His hair stuck out in all directions and his face was fresh with pillow creases.

"Come sit next to me, sweetie." Caitlyn tapped her hand on the empty chair.

Henry took sluggish steps toward Caitlyn and flopped down into the seat. "You're going to say no because it's not on your list." He frowned and pointed to the open journal.

"Not exactly. If we have time today, we can stop by the pond. This morning I thought I'd take you out for breakfast at the Hummingbird Café. I know how much you love French toast and Miss Nellie said theirs is the best."

"So we can go to the pond after?" Henry sat a little straighter.

"After breakfast we're going over to the Garrisons' so I can help Miss Nellie cook for the church potluck supper tomorrow. I told you about it yesterday, remember?"

Henry's slumped posture returned. "Yeah, but you can't cook."

"It's not that I can't. I just don't really like it that much. But Miss Nellie is going to teach me how to make her special country-fried steak, and I'm going to bake brownies." Caitlyn snuggled up close to Henry. "Come on, it will be fun. Mr. Garrison said he'll take you out to their barn. You can help him feed his sheep. He even said he'd teach you how to milk their dairy cow, Betty."

No response. Normally, any mention of animals would perk Henry up and he'd be ready to go. But Donald consumed his thoughts. "After we're finished at the Garrisons', if there's still time, we'll make a stop at the pond. How does that sound?"

"Okay, I guess," Henry mumbled.

"Now go get dressed and brush your teeth. We'll head out for breakfast once you're finished."

Henry's chair screeched as he pushed away from the table. He stood but made no movement to get ready for the day.

"Sweetie, are you okay?" Henry's blank stare caused Caitlyn's heart rate to quicken. Was he having a seizure? This was often one of the first warning signs.

"Yeah. I just miss Donald. I'm afraid she's hurt." Henry turned and left the kitchen.

Caitlyn's heartbeat slowed, but her worries remained. That darn duck. If Donald didn't turn up soon, Caitlyn wasn't sure how she would convince Henry to stop worrying.

An hour later, Caitlyn and Henry stepped into the Hummingbird Café. Henry had barely spoken on the ride over. Caitlyn hoped it was because he was still sleepy. With the perfect weather, she took a seat at the bistro table outside.

"Good morning, welcome to the Hummingbird Café."

Caitlyn looked up at the older woman who'd offered the friendly welcome. "Thank you. This is our first time here." Caitlyn tilted her head toward the ball pit where Henry was laughing. Her shoulders relaxed.

"Is that your son?" the woman asked.

"Yes, that's Henry."

"I'm the owner—Sally Raphine." She extended her hand.

"Caitlyn Calloway," she said with a smile.

"Oh, yes, I've heard all about you. I'm sorry I haven't been able to come over to help with the renovations. The restaurant keeps me pretty busy."

Caitlyn waved her hand. "Please don't even think about that. I'm grateful to everyone in the town. They've gone above and beyond to help me get the house ready to sell." Caitlyn could never repay them for their kindness.

"So what I've heard is true? You're going to sell the property?" Sally's pleasantness seemed to fade. "I thought since it was your childhood home, you might change your mind."

Caitlyn considered the woman's remarks. If she stayed in Bluebell much longer, her decision to leave would only become more difficult. Henry's growing attachment to the town and its people caused her concern. "No, that's not an option. My life and my business are in Wyoming."

Sally pulled a stubby pencil with no eraser from behind her ear, along with the pad of paper from the pocket on her apron. "I understand. Now, what can I get you?"

"Henry will have an order of your famous French toast."

"And what would you like?"

The discussion about going home had soured Caitlyn's appetite. "I'll just have some black coffee, thank you."

Sally nodded. "Let me know if you change your mind. I'll be back with Henry's food shortly." Sally hurried off to the elderly couple who took a seat at the opposite end of the patio.

Caitlyn considered Sally's remarks. She realized Bluebell was the perfect place to raise Henry. But how could she uproot her business and move? If she didn't sell Last Dollar, how would she be able to pay off all the medical bills and past-due rent? She couldn't leave Wyoming without making things right with her landlord. Considering such a move would only distract her from the plan to get the house ready to sell.

Caitlyn gazed over at the ball pit. Henry was playing with a little boy and girl who looked to be his age. Her heart squeezed, watching him frolic among the colorful balls. Even if it was for the moment, thoughts of Donald were far from his mind, and he was enjoying just being a little boy. With Henry's birthday coming up the last week of June, maybe she could bring him to the café to celebrate.

"Good morning. This is a pleasant surprise."

The familiar, deep masculine voice drew Caitlyn's attention from Henry. She looked up. Logan towered over her table, dressed in jeans and a T-shirt. He tipped the brim of his cowboy hat.

"Do you mind if I join you?" he asked.

Caitlyn's response to Logan's casual appearance was a little unnerving. Lately, the more she was around him equated to wanting more time with him. That couldn't be a good thing. "Of course, please, have a seat."

Logan slipped into the chair next to hers. His clean scent caught up in the breeze. He sure smelled good. She wished she'd taken the time to make herself a little more presentable. If she'd known she was going to see Logan, she might have even put on a touch of makeup.

Logan tilted his head toward the ball pit. "It looks like Henry's having a good time."

"Yes, he is now. I had to drag him here and bribe him with French toast."

"Well, you brought him to the right place. Sally has the best French toast in the state."

Caitlyn nodded. "That's what I hear."

"So why wasn't Henry interested in breakfast this morning?"

"I'll give you one guess." Caitlyn gave a forced smile.

"Donald."

Caitlyn nodded her head. "He can't get his mind off of her. I think part of the reason he didn't want to come for breakfast is because his stomach has been upset the last few days. At first I thought he had a stomach bug, but then I realized the poor little guy is worrying himself sick over Donald's disappearance. Do you think she'll come back to the pond?"

Logan shrugged his shoulders. "It's hard to say. It's been her home for quite a while, so unless she got injured during the storm, I can't see her not returning."

"I need to get his mind focused on something other than that duck." She gave him a look with hopes of an answer.

"What's on your agenda for today?"

Caitlyn explained her plans to help Nellie with the church potluck supper. "I'd hoped Henry would be happy to spend some time with the Garrisons' farm animals today, but even that didn't get him excited."

Logan paused for a moment. "I'd like to run something by you, but think about it before you answer. Either way, you won't hurt my feelings."

Caitlyn couldn't imagine what Logan had in mind. She was desperate. "What is it?"

"How about after breakfast I take Henry over to my house? I planned to work with Sophie for a couple of hours this morning. Next week, she transitions to her new handler, so I have to make sure she's ready for the job. It might be good for Henry to learn what's involved with training a dog."

Caitlyn's first instinct was thanks but no thanks. After the hailstorm drama, she was uncomfortable letting Henry out of her sight. But she knew that was unrealistic, especially when they head home to Wyoming and he went back to school. The bigger reason for her hesitation was spending time with Logan. Henry longed for a father figure. In Henry's eyes, Logan was the perfect person to fill those shoes. Honestly, the more time with Logan, Caitlyn was feeling the same—another reason to say no.

Silence lingered at the table before Logan spoke again. "So? What do you think?"

Caitlyn twisted a strand of hair. "I don't know—with his stomach and all."

Logan laughed. "What if we make a deal?"

"What's that?" Caitlyn wasn't sure about making another deal with Logan.

"If Henry shows any signs of feeling sick, or not wanting to be with me and Sophie after fifteen minutes, I'll bring him back over to the Garrisons'? If he's having a good time and wants to stay, we can meet up at Mr. Pepperoni for lunch. Around one o'clock? Or you can text me when you're finished cooking with Nellie."

Caitlyn glanced in Henry's direction. He was still enjoying time with his new friends. For the past twenty minutes, Henry hadn't displayed signs of any stomach ailment. Instead, he was just having fun for a change. Caitlyn turned back to Logan.

"Come on, what do you say?"

A gorgeous smile parted his lips and she caved. How could she say no to such a generous offer? The man obviously had a busy schedule, but he wanted to take the time out of his day to help Henry—to help her. Just like everyone else in Bluebell. With each day that passed, the love she felt from this town continued to tug at her heartstrings. "Okay, but first we have to ask Henry."

Logan nodded. "You're the boss."

Moments later, Sally brought Henry's breakfast to the table, along with her cup of coffee.

"Hi, Logan. It's good to see you this morning. Would you like some breakfast?"

"Hey, Sal. You know me. I will never say no to your French toast. I'll have that with a side order of hash browns and a large black coffee, please."

"You got it." Sally hurried back to the kitchen to put in the order.

Caitlyn motioned for Henry to come and eat. At first, he hesitated, but when he saw Logan at the table, he flashed a big grin and climbed out of the ball pit. He waved goodbye to his friends and raced over.

"Hi, Mr. Logan! I didn't know you were going to be here!" Henry pulled out a chair in front of his breakfast and flopped down. "Any sign of Donald?"

Caitlyn expelled a heavy breath. The ball pit had proved to only be a temporary distraction from Henry's fixation on Donald.

"No, not yet, but be patient. I think she'll come around."

"But it's been a long time since the storm," Henry said.

"Give her time, buddy. Did you have fun over there?"

"Yeah, but those kids had to go soon. Their mom and dad are taking them to the zoo in Denver."

Caitlyn's ears perked up. "That sounds like fun. Maybe we can do that before we go back to Wyoming." Caitlyn noticed Henry's expression sadden. He wasn't in a hurry to go back home. Especially if he couldn't see Donald before he left.

"Yeah, the zoo in the city is pretty cool, but your mom told me you're going to see some animals yourself today." Logan turned to Henry. "The Garrisons have quite a few critters. I think you'll enjoy your visit."

Henry shrugged his shoulders. "Yeah, I guess it'll be okay, but I'd rather be out looking for Donald."

"Well, if you're not excited about going to the Garrisons', maybe you'd like to come with me." Logan paused when Henry bounced up and down in his chair.

"Yes! I'd rather go with you."

Caitlyn and Logan laughed at the same time.

"You don't even know where I'm going," Logan said.

"I don't care. Anywhere you go is fine with me as long as we're together."

Caitlyn's heart squeezed. She could feel Logan's eyes on her. Was she wrong in allowing this attachment Henry had for Logan to grow stronger? And if it was wrong, what did she plan to do about it? But she had an even bigger problem. What on earth did she plan to do about her own growing attachment to Logan?

Henry took a leap from the back seat of Logan's pickup. He turned with a giant smile. "Your truck is the coolest! Mom never drives with all the windows down. That was fun!"

Logan laughed and rested his hand on Henry's shoulder. "That's the best way to listen to country music—turned up, with the windows open, while driving down a country road. It's my favorite way to clear my mind."

"Clear your mind?" Henry looked up.

Logan would like nothing better than for Henry to live his life problem free. To have his biggest worry be a missing duck. But that wasn't how life worked. "You know how sometimes your head gets full of so many things you can't think straight?"

"Yeah, I know what you mean," Henry responded, sounding older than his years.

"How old are you again?" Logan joked.

"I'll be eight in three weeks," he announced proudly.

Logan made a mental note to ask Caitlyn if she had anything planned for Henry's birthday. If she gave the okay, there was nothing he'd like more than to throw him a surprise party. The kid needed some fun in his life. "So, what's on your mind these days, buddy?"

"Donald."

"What else?" Logan was curious what filled Henry's thoughts.

"Since Mom inherited the house, I keep thinking how cool it would be if we could move here. Every time I mention it to her, she tells me it's impossible. Do you think so?"

Logan didn't want to contradict anything Caitlyn had said to Henry. "Let me turn that question around to you." Logan challenged Henry, "Do you think it's impossible?"

Henry bit on his lower lip and crinkled his brow. "Before we came to Bluebell, I learned in Sunday school nothing is impossible with God. Would it be wrong for me to pray that Mom changes her mind and keeps the house so we can live here?"

Funny, after spending so much time with Caitlyn, Logan had prayed for the same thing last night. "If that's what's in your heart, it's not wrong. The more you can reveal your heart to God, the more he'll understand what's best for you."

"So I can keep praying that Mom will change her mind?"

Logan turned and reached for Henry's hand to head toward the paddock. "I think that would be okay."

Logan didn't share his heart with Henry, but he planned to continue praying for the same thing.

Once inside the gated area, Sophie ran straight to Henry.

"Sophie is such a cool dog. I'd love to have one like

her." Henry giggled as the dog covered his hands in sloppy kisses.

"Maybe one day you will, but you have to make sure you're ready to handle all the responsibilities that come with dog ownership."

"You mean like feeding it and walking it?"

Logan nodded. "Yes, but taking care of a dog involves more than that. If you're going to be a dog owner, you want to train the dog yourself or by a professional."

"Like you? Maybe if Mom lets me get a dog, I can let you train it," Henry suggested. "How long have you been training Sophie?"

The first day the volunteer puppy-raiser had brought Sophie to the ranch, Logan had fallen in love with her. He'd realized instantly she had the intelligence and temperament to be a great service dog. "I've been training Sophie formally for the last several months."

"Wow! She must know a lot by now."

"She's been a quick learner, haven't you, girl?"

Sophie barked and Logan reached to give her a good head rub.

"Aren't you training her to be somebody's eyes?"

"You're exactly right."

"What did you teach her first?" Henry fired off another question.

Logan liked Henry's curiosity. "First, I did the basic obedience training and taught her how to respond to verbal and physical cues. Once she learned those skills, I taught her how to navigate safely in different environments. Since the handler of Sophie won't be able to see what's around her, I had to train the dog how to stop at curbs, steps and other potential hazards."

Henry got down on the ground in front of Sophie. "You

must be really smart." Sophie responded by covering Henry's face with wet kisses. Henry giggled. "When do you have to give her to that lady?"

Logan was confident Sophie was more than ready to take over the role of a professional service dog. "I take her to Denver next week."

Henry scratched Sophie underneath her chin. The dog flopped to the ground, rolled over onto her back, her legs up, and wiggled, waiting for a belly rub. Henry complied. "Isn't it hard to give the dogs away to strangers? I hardly know Sophie and I don't want her to leave. I can't imagine how you must feel."

Henry was an intuitive little boy. "You're right, it is difficult to let go of a dog after you've spent so much time with them. But it makes me happy to know all the good the dog will do for their new handler by enhancing their independence and safety. Keeping all of that in mind makes it a lot easier to say goodbye."

"That's cool you help people like that," Henry said.

Logan joined Henry on the ground and rubbed Sophie's stomach. She thanked him by wiggling faster and licking his hand. "Sophie is the one who does all the work and will continue to work hard. I only get her started off with the proper training."

"Boy, I sure wish I lived here. You could teach me everything you know and I could help you." A melancholy smile tugged at the corners of Henry's mouth.

If Logan could purchase the land from Caitlyn, he could use an enthusiastic helper like Henry to move forward with his dream. Logan plucked a blade of grass from the ground and stuck it between his teeth. "Can I let you in on a little secret?"

Henry's eyes widened. "Sure! I'm great at keeping secrets.

As long as it's not anything against the law or anything that might hurt somebody, I guess it's okay not to tell my mom."

Logan laughed. "You're right. There are certain things you should never keep from your mother. This is a different secret. It's more of a dream." Once he'd shared his idea with his brothers, it was no longer a secret. Both Jake and Cody had been excited and supportive about Logan's potential business venture. They'd offered to help in any way they could.

"Like my dream to move here?"

Logan nodded. "Exactly like that."

Henry crossed his heart. "I promise I won't tell anybody."

"Okay, then. You know how I told you I rescued Sophie from an organization before I trained her?"

"Yeah, I remember. We had people like that come to our school one day. The lady told us they save dogs' lives. She said some people get a dog and then decide they don't want it anymore, so they just let it loose. The rescue place gets the dog adopted before something bad happens to them." Henry paused for a moment and crinkled his brow. He turned to Logan. "Did you know my mom adopted me?"

"Yes, your mother mentioned it," Logan answered.

"I don't know what would've happened to me if she didn't, so I think adoption is a good thing for kids and for dogs." Henry smile was wistful.

Logan patted Henry on the leg. "You're right. It's a wonderful thing. That's where my dream comes in to play. I'd like to start a rescue organization to save and rehabilitate a larger number of dogs. By training these dogs to assist people with disabilities, or by improving their chances of finding suitable homes, I can make a positive impact. There's nothing like that available to residents in Bluebell or the surrounding communities. I'd like to educate the community about responsible dog ownership, animal welfare, and the importance of adopting rather than buying a dog. There are a lot of myths associated with shelter animals."

"Yeah, that's what the lady told our class. She said some people think no one wants the dogs because they're mean and stuff."

"She's right, but it doesn't mean the animal shouldn't have an opportunity at a second chance." Logan smiled. It was apparent Henry had listened to the representative who'd visited his class.

"Yeah, my mom gave me a second chance."

Logan admired Caitlyn for opening her heart and her home to Henry. "Your mom is pretty amazing."

Henry mimicked Logan, pulling on a piece of grass and putting it between his teeth. "I think she likes you. Maybe you should ask her on a date."

The thought had crossed Logan's mind several times over the last couple of days. There'd been moments when they were together that he'd believed she might say yes if he asked her out to dinner, but Caitlyn had her mind set on leaving Bluebell. Why bother starting something that would ultimately end? "I like your mother, too, but we're just friends.

"Why don't we take Sophie for a walk down to the pond?" Logan needed to get his mind off the idea of going on a date with Caitlyn. As much as he'd love for that to happen, it wasn't in the cards.

Henry sprang to his feet. "Yeah, maybe Donald will be back."

After a short walk, they arrived at the water. Logan and Henry scanned the area, but there was no sign of Donald.

Henry's shoulders slumped. "She's not here. I don't think she's ever coming back."

For several minutes, they stood quietly.

"Are you okay, buddy?" Logan asked.

Henry's body trembled and his eyes widened as he staggered closer to the water's edge.

Logan's eyes narrowed. "Henry! Can you tell me what's wrong?"

The boy's breath became ragged and his face turned pale.

Sophie moved closer to Henry and whimpered.

Logan dropped to his knees beside Henry. He yanked his cell phone from his pocket to call Olivia. Logan quickly scrolled through his contacts and pressed her name. He prayed she wasn't with a patient.

She picked up.

"Olivia! It's Logan. I'm at the pond with Henry, Caitlyn's boy. He's having some sort of seizure. I'm not sure what to do. Can you come?" Logan paused and inhaled.

"Of course," Olivia responded, her tone urgent. "But check his body for any type of medical alert identification. A bracelet or necklace."

Logan scanned his arm and then pulled Henry's T-shirt away from his neck. "There's a necklace!" Logan pulled on the chain and read the silver medallion. "He has epilepsy!"

"Remove the necklace and get him safely on the ground. Make sure there aren't any objects close by that he can grab and injure himself. Try to keep him on his side until I get there," Olivia instructed. "And, Logan, stay calm. The seizure should subside on its own."

The line went silent.

Logan followed his sister-in-law's directions. His heart pounded against his chest as Henry's symptoms continued. A mix of guilt and fear consumed Logan.

Why hadn't Caitlyn told him Henry had epilepsy?

Chapter Eleven

Caitlyn ran up the front steps to Logan's house. Her heart pounded against her chest. When she'd received Logan's frantic phone call while cooking with Nellie, it had taken her back to the first time she'd witnessed Henry having a seizure. Guilt settled in. She should have told Logan about Henry's medical background. But she'd wanted to protect her son. He didn't want people to treat him differently because of the epilepsy, especially Kyle and Kayla. Henry only wanted to be like other kids.

Caitlyn rushed through the front door without knocking. "Where is he?" she cried.

Logan stepped into the foyer. "You can relax. He's okay. Olivia is with him in the guest room. Remember, she's the town doctor, so he's in excellent hands."

"Please take me to him. I'd like to see him."

As they neared the door to the guest room, Olivia stepped out into the hall. She pulled the door behind her, leaving it slightly ajar. "He's sleeping like a baby now." Olivia looked at Caitlyn. "Don't worry. He was breathing fine and talking normally before he drifted off to sleep. I think Logan may be the one who needs medical attention. He was white as a sheet when I got to the pond." Olivia patted Logan on his arm.

Caitlyn moved to the door and peeked through the crack. Just as Olivia had said, Henry was sleeping soundly. She stepped toward Olivia and reached for her hands. "Thank you so much for taking care of him." Her eyes shifted on Logan. "Please accept my apology. I should have told you about the epilepsy before allowing you to be alone with Henry. I know how frightening it can be to witness a seizure when you don't know what's happening."

Silence hung in the air.

"I'm going to grab my bag and head on out. Logan has my number. Call if you need anything else," Olivia said.

"Thanks for coming, Liv," Logan said before Olivia headed back into the bedroom to retrieve her medical bag.

"Why don't we step out to the kitchen? I could use a cup of coffee," Logan suggested.

A few minutes later, Caitlyn and Logan sat at the kitchen table, each with a cup of coffee.

"I can make a fresh pot if you'd like," Caitlyn offered.

Logan took a quick sip. "No, this is fine. Thanks."

Outside, the car door slammed and the motor started as Olivia left the property.

"I can't tell you how thankful I am to Olivia." Caitlyn hesitated for a moment before reaching across the table and placing her hand on Logan's arm. "I'm thankful for you, too. Again, I apologize for not being up front with you. Henry has such a difficult time with kids bullying and excluding him."

"That's a shame. Kids can be so cruel," Logan said.

"Yes, they can. But if you don't know what's happening, witnessing someone having a seizure for the first time can be terrifying, as you experienced firsthand. Henry doesn't want to be different from other children, so he denies he has limitations. Earlier this year, before we got him on a new medication to help reduce the frequency and duration of the seizures, he had a lot of challenges at school. After having several seizures in the classroom, his classmates became frightened of being around him. The last thing I want is for Henry to be defined by his medical condition. I only want him to have a normal childhood."

"Have you ever considered getting Henry a seizure dog?" Logan asked.

"I don't know if that would benefit Henry." Last year, Caitlyn had done a little research, but once she'd seen the costs involved, she hadn't bothered to educate herself any further.

"I train seizure dogs to recognize the signs and symptoms of an impending seizure. The dog can often detect a change in the child's behavior and body language before a seizure occurs. By alerting the child or those around them, the dog can provide a warning which allows the child to take necessary precautions or to seek a safe environment."

"Interesting—could you tell me a little more?" Caitlyn asked.

"They serve a variety of purposes. For example, during a seizure, the dog can offer physical support and comfort. They can lie next to the child to prevent injury, provide a sense of security, and help reduce anxiety and fear. I can even train the animal to activate alarms or devices that can alert caregivers or emergency services for help."

"That's incredible." Training for a dog like Logan described would cost a fortune. Perhaps once she paid off her debt, she could afford to look into it.

"The dog can also be trained to go for help, like what happened today. If Henry was at the pond by himself, a seizure dog can find a trusted adult or caregiver and lead them back to the child. This can be especially helpful if the child is disoriented or unable to communicate their needs effectively."

"Well, that would never happen. I wouldn't allow Henry to go to the pond alone—or anywhere." Caitlyn knew many people saw her as overprotective, especially Henry, but she had good reason to be. Today was a perfect example.

"What about when Henry gets a little older? You can't follow him everywhere he goes. At some point, he'll need a chance to exercise his independence."

"I'm not sure Henry is ready for that." Caitlyn folded her arms against her chest.

"It's not my intention to push anything on you. I guess I'm surprised you wouldn't be more open to the idea, especially after mentioning being impressed by the news story about me."

Caitlyn remained silent.

"A seizure dog can offer Henry constant companionship and emotional support. You said it yourself. Henry doesn't feel like he has friends. The dog can provide comfort during times of stress or anxiety related to epilepsy. Having a loving and nonjudgmental companion can help reduce his feelings of isolation as well as promote a sense of security and well-being."

Caitlyn shook her head. "I'm sorry, Logan. It's not my intention to belittle what you do. I know you and your brothers help many people and your company does amazing things. It's just—" Caitlyn paused.

"You don't want to draw attention to Henry's limitations, right?" Logan said.

"Well, no, I don't. I think bringing a dog into the classroom or out in public places will only bring more attention to Henry. That's the last thing that he wants." Caitlyn ran her finger around the rim of her coffee cup.

Logan straightened his shoulders. "The last thing he wants or the last thing you want? Be honest."

Caitlyn's mouth fell open.

"I'm sorry. I was out of line. It's just a common initial reaction by both the handler and their family. No one wants to draw attention to their disability, but the reality is there should be more focus on individuals with special needs. The more educated, the better we can understand the need and perhaps exhibit more empathy. Kids might not be as frightened if they know what happens during a seizure. On the first day of school, if Henry had come into the classroom with a trained seizure dog, the teacher and Henry could have explained why the animal was there and the purpose it served. Then the children would have a better understanding when and if a seizure occurred in the classroom."

Caitlyn listened but didn't respond.

Logan cleared his throat and leaned forward. "I'll say one last thing and then I'll drop it. Introducing a seizure dog as part of Henry's therapy could enhance the quality of his life. It could encourage greater participation in activities he might otherwise avoid due to fear of seizures."

The sound of a door creaking echoed down the hallway.

Caitlyn looked at Logan. "Thank you for educating me on seizure dogs, but I don't think that is something Henry needs right now. Besides, he's too young to handle a dog."

Logan simply nodded.

Caitlyn was relieved Logan didn't push the issue. "Please don't mention this in front of Henry. As you know, he loves dogs. If he thought I was even considering bringing a dog into our home, he'd pester me to death."

"Of course, I won't say anything. But I still hope that you'll give it more consideration. It really could be life-changing for Henry."

Logan had a valid point. After listening to him explain the benefits of a seizure dog, it was clear to Caitlyn that a service animal would help Henry. But the reality of the situation stared her in the face. Owning a dog cost money, especially a trained service dog. Given her current circumstances, keeping a roof over their heads was her top priority.

"Hi." Henry entered the kitchen, rubbing his eyes. "I woke up and wasn't sure where I was."

"The doctor and Mr. Logan brought you to his house." Caitlyn jumped up out of the chair. "Are you feeling better, sweetie? Why don't you sit down with us? I can get you some water or juice if you'd like."

Logan stood. "I've got some orange soda—if it's okay with your mother."

"That would be fine." Caitlyn took Henry's hand and guided him to the kitchen table.

Henry stopped in front of Logan. "Hey, buddy. I'm glad to see you up."

Henry looked down at the floor before glancing up at Logan. "I'm sorry for what happened earlier. I didn't mean to scare you."

Logan placed a hand on Henry's shoulder. "I know you didn't. You're okay, and that's all that matters now. Have a seat and I'll get you some soda."

Henry remained standing. "I didn't want Kayla and Kyle to know I have epilepsy. That's why I didn't tell you. We've been having so much fun together. I'm afraid if they find out, they'll stop liking me."

Caitlyn's heart squeezed for her son. She would do anything to cure Henry. It wasn't fair that he had to deal with this kind of challenge.

"You don't have to worry about Kayla and Kyle. You can tell them you have epilepsy. They are your friends, no matter what."

Henry glanced at his mother before looking back at Logan.

"I guess they can be my friends until we go back home. I don't like it there. No one wants to be my friend. Everybody is scared to be around me."

"Oh, sweetie. I know it feels like that, but once people get to know you and learn a little more about epilepsy, they're not afraid of you. Kids that don't want to be your friend just because you have a seizure now and then don't deserve your friendship. You're a special person. Never forget that."

"I don't want to be special." Henry sat down at the table and frowned. "I just want to be like everybody else."

Logan and Caitlyn exchanged glances. It wasn't uncommon for Henry to experience these meltdowns after a seizure. Caitlyn had learned to let it run its course and eventually Henry would bounce back.

Caitlyn checked her watch. "I did not know it was this late in the day. I'm sorry if we kept you from doing what you usually do on Saturday."

"No, you're fine. Like I told Henry earlier, Sophie's trained and ready to go to her handler, so the rest of my day is free." Logan rubbed his stomach. "I don't know about the two of you, but I'm starving."

Having only coffee for breakfast and skipping lunch while helping at Nellie's house, Caitlyn's stomach grumbled at the mention of food. "I could definitely eat," she said.

"I'm hungry, too," Henry chirped.

"How about I drive us all into town for pizza?" Logan offered.

"Yum! I vote yes!" Henry jumped up and down.

"Pizza it is." Caitlyn glanced at Henry and laughed.

Logan leaned toward Caitlyn. "You'd never know he'd just experienced a seizure."

"That's how they are, sometimes, gone as quickly as they come."

They stepped outside and the gentle breeze stirred Caitlyn's thoughts. The idea of a service dog held the promise of transforming Henry's life. Deep down, Caitlyn knew Logan was right. Her heart sank with a mix of emotions as the truth gnawed at her conscience. A veil of secrecy covered the reality of her situation and prevented her from disclosing the real obstacle standing in the way. Waiting for her at home in Wyoming was a suffocating mountain of debt.

Friday morning, the first rays of sunlight painted the sky in pink and gold. Logan loved the tranquil stillness of the ranch in the early morning hours. It was a perfect morning for a horseback ride. The rhythmic sounds of hooves hitting the ground filled the air. Logan glanced at his younger brother, Cody, and tightened the reins on his chestnut quarter horse, Buck. The horse was a gift to Logan from Melody.

"Are you sure that's a good idea?" Cody asked. "Caitlyn told you she didn't think Henry was ready for a seizure service dog."

Late Wednesday night, Logan had texted Cody to invite him on an early morning trail ride. Since his conversation with Caitlyn last Saturday about the benefits of a seizure dog, Logan hadn't been able to get it off his mind. Why was Caitlyn so resistant?

"I know that's what she said, but I don't think she understands the true benefits. Henry's a great kid, but his self-esteem is low. He feels so isolated by the seizures, he's attached himself to a duck because it's different, like him."

"Donald?" Cody tilted his head.

"Yeah. From the first day Henry spotted Donald in the pond and noticed she differed from the other ducks, he's been obsessed. He's been worried sick about her because we haven't seen her since the hailstorm."

"The poor kid. So let me guess. The reason you brought me here this morning is to talk about Cooper. Am I right?" Cody shifted his Stetson as the sun climbed higher in the sky.

Over the last few months, Cody had been working with the two-year-old labradoodle. A friend working for a service dog organization in Denver had reached out for more specialized training. Cody was happy to oblige, since his friend had offered support and help over the years. "Has your friend found a partner for the dog?"

"Not yet. Initially, I was training Cooper for a woman in Colorado Springs, but she recently had to back out. She said it was for personal reasons, so I didn't want to pry. I'm going forward with Cooper's training. We agreed whoever needs a partner first, Cooper would go to that person," Cody explained.

God had a hand in all of this. Cooper was available and practically fully trained to work as a seizure dog, and Henry could benefit. The timing couldn't be more perfect. "If I finish up with Cooper's training, can I choose the partner?" Logan glanced at his brother.

Cody laughed and shook his head. "You don't give up, do you? Are you sure you want to do this?" Cody flashed his eyes on his brother. "Going against her wishes might not be the best way to get her to go on a date with you."

"Who said anything about me asking her on a date?" Logan was aware of his growing feelings for Caitlyn, but had they been that obvious to his brother? Maybe so. Even little Henry had mentioned a date.

Cody flashed a mischievous grin. "Come on, buddy. Let's be honest. It's like you've got a giant neon sign hanging above your head. 'I'm head over heels for Caitlyn Calloway!'" he exclaimed, unable to suppress his laughter. "Jake and I were just talking about it on Sunday. We were watching the two of you at the potluck supper. Even Nellie can see it."

Nellie? Logan's stomach knotted. How would she know? Of course, Logan was well aware of the fact that Nellie knew everything that happened in Bluebell. "You all are imagining things. Caitlyn and I have a business relationship, that's all."

"It's obvious to me and probably everyone else within a ten-mile radius that you've fallen hard for Caitlyn. It's about time you opened up that big heart of yours. You've got a lot of love to give. Melody would want you to move on and to be happy."

Falling for Caitlyn once again was the last thing Logan had expected. Of course, the first time it had merely been a secret crush, but now, as much as he tried to fight it, Caitlyn had found her way back into his heart. He couldn't deny it—but he had to. Her plan was to return to Wyoming. As far as Logan could tell, when Caitlyn had a plan, she stuck to it. "Maybe so, but Caitlyn will leave as soon as she sells the house." Logan's heart sank at the thought. "Now, can we get back to the reason I brought you out here?"

"Right—Cooper. So, you really want to do this?"

Logan couldn't shake the lingering suspicion. Did Caitlyn's hesitation to get a service dog for Henry stem from her financial situation? Several instances flashed through his mind. Caitlyn hunched over her journal while she meticulously calculated repair costs and wrestled with the financial burden of readying the farmhouse to put on the market. "The other day, Henry mentioned he had a birthday coming up at the end of the month. I can't think of a more perfect gift."

Cody laughed. "Well, it's your call. If that's what you

want to do, Cooper won't require much additional training. He's been a fast learner."

"Since I took Sophie up to Denver on Tuesday, the timing couldn't be more perfect."

"So, how do you plan to handle this gift? Are you just going to spring it on her?" Cody asked.

"I've thought about it, and I have an idea. I'm going to call her today and ask her if she has plans for Henry's birthday. It's coming up two weeks from Saturday. I'd like to host a surprise party for him at my house. I'm going to talk to Olivia today about having Kayla and Kyle invite some children from town. From what I gather, he doesn't have a lot of friends back home in Wyoming."

"A party sounds like a great idea. I can't imagine Caitlyn would say no. I can help you out with anything you need."

"Thanks. I'll probably take you up on that." Logan could always count on Cody.

"Still, I have my doubts about springing Cooper on Caitlyn at the party. What if she says no and Henry has already met the dog? He'll be heartbroken."

Logan agreed with Cody. The last thing he'd ever do was cause Henry any pain. "Look, I haven't figured out all the logistics of it, but one thing I can guarantee is I will discuss it with Caitlyn before Henry ever sees Cooper."

Logan and Cody rode in silence as they made their way back to the stable. With only the horses' hooves echoing across the tranquil countryside, Logan was at peace with his decision to go forward with his plan. Logan hoped to ease any financial concerns for Caitlyn. He wanted to help her recognize the positive impact Cooper could have on Henry's well-being. Logan was more determined than ever to help Caitlyn, the woman who'd captured his heart for the second time in his life.

Chapter Twelve

Early Saturday morning, Caitlyn was up before daylight with a glimmer of hope and an extra pep in her step. The past week had been a whirlwind filled with good news. Repairs on Last Dollar were moving along. Caitlyn finally saw a promise of light at the end of the tunnel. Thanks to Logan's determination and the help of a few volunteers, the roof repair was on the schedule for next week. If everything went well, Caitlyn hoped to have the house on the market after the Fourth of July. According to the real estate agent, it was a perfect time to sell since potential homebuyers like to be settled before the start of a new school year.

Besides the good news on the repairs, there'd been a heartwarming surprise. One that created a feeling of weightlessness each time it graced her mind.

Last week, a call from Logan that wasn't about the repairs on Last Dollar had caught Caitlyn off guard. He had offered to throw a surprise party for Henry. Logan had explained how after Henry had mentioned in passing that he had a birthday coming up, he couldn't get it off his mind. Henry deserved to have a surprise party thrown in his honor with all of his new friends from Bluebell in attendance. Logan's thoughtfulness overwhelmed Caitlyn. The only problem was how would she be able to keep it a secret for the next two weeks? Henry was a curious little boy, and he always seemed to have his eyes and ears open to catch items.

Footsteps pitter-pattered in the hall, heading toward the kitchen. Caitlyn glanced up from her cup of black coffee and journal. She pushed her chair away from the table and stood, placing her hand to her chest. Henry came toward her, already dressed for the day.

"Well, isn't this a nice surprise? I thought I'd have to drag you out of bed this morning since you stayed up past your bedtime last night."

Henry smiled. "It was fun. Thanks for letting me stay up later to watch the movie. The popcorn was good, too. I liked the cinnamon you sprinkled on it."

Caitlyn's heart warmed. Last evening had meant so much to her. It was a special night and one that was long overdue. Lately, all Caitlyn thought about were repairs in need of attention, a depleting bank account, past-due rent and getting out of Bluebell as fast as she could. Last night proved that she'd lost sight of what was truly important. Creating special moments with her son was what mattered most. "I'm happy you had a good time. I think we need to do that more often, don't you?"

Henry ran across the room and wrapped his arms around her waist. The day she'd signed the adoption papers flashed in her mind. The opportunity to be Henry's mother had been an extraordinary gift from God. Each passing day brought Caitlyn a sense of joy beyond measure. Providing Henry with love and a stable future was a priority. It was the reason she got out of bed each morning.

"Maybe we can do it every Friday night?" Henry looked up with a grin that revealed another missing tooth.

"That sounds like a great idea." Caitlyn cupped Henry's

chin with her left hand and touched his lower lip with her right index finger. "Hey, what's this?"

Henry giggled. "I almost forgot to tell you. My front tooth fell out this morning."

"I see that." Caitlyn tickled his stomach. "You'll have to be sure and put it under your pillow tonight."

"I will." Henry flopped down on the chair. "Maybe it was all of that popcorn that shook it loose."

Caitlyn laughed. "Maybe so, but I think it's because you're getting older." A part of Caitlyn would like to keep Henry at this age so he'd never grow up and leave her to have a life of his own, but that was silly. "Speaking of—I know someone who has a birthday coming up." She slid into the chair beside Henry's.

The room grew silent except for the faint hum of the refrigerator.

"Well, aren't you excited?" Henry's lack of interest in his upcoming birthday concerned Caitlyn.

Henry shrugged his shoulders. "Not really. It's just another day."

Caitlyn's heart sank. "Not to me, it's not. It's your special day. Last year you started dropping hints about birthday presents a month before. What's different this year?"

Henry squirmed in the chair. "I only want two things, but I don't think I'll get either." He put his elbows up on the kitchen table and placed his hands to his cheeks.

Caitlyn was afraid to ask why he wasn't excited about his upcoming birthday. What if she couldn't fulfill Henry's birthday wishes? Whatever it was, she'd do everything in her power to make this year his best. She drew in a breath and released. "Do you want to give me a hint?"

"The only thing I want for my birthday is to see Donald before we leave. I miss her so much." Henry looked to the bay window, as though hoping to see Donald waddle up onto the back patio.

Caitlyn had had a feeling Donald would be one of the two wishes. Unfortunately, she didn't know how to bring the duck back. Logan had assured her that eventually Donald would return to the pond. But how could he be so sure? What if by the time the duck came back she and Henry are long gone? Maybe she could fulfill his second wish. "What's the other, sweetie?" She held her breath.

Henry paused. "To never leave Bluebell," he blurted. "I wish we could move into Last Dollar and make it our home, like it was yours when you were little. Please. Why can't we?"

"I've explained why that's not possible, sweetie." The joy she and Henry had experienced the night before was now a distant memory, replaced by the challenges of life. Caitlyn wanted nothing more than to give Henry everything his little heart desired. "Would you like pancakes for your breakfast? We have time before I take you over to the Garrisons'." Caitlyn needed something to keep her mind busy.

The plan was to speak with Nellie in private about Henry's epilepsy before dropping him off to help her with the store inventory. She and Logan would then meet in secret about Henry's birthday party. That's what she kept telling herself, but her heart tried to convince her that this meeting was something more.

Henry looked up. His hair nearly covered one eye. "Can I have chocolate chips?"

Caitlyn made a mental note to add "get Henry's hair cut before the party" to her to-do list tucked inside her journal. "Of course you can."

"Do you think after I finish helping Mrs. Garrison in the store, Mr. Garrison will let me play with some of their animals? He told me the other day they were getting a couple more baby goats." He stared off into the air. "I sure wish we could get a goat."

"I'm sure you'll be able to play with the animals. Just promise me you'll be on your best behavior." Her gentle reminder wasn't necessary. People often complimented her on Henry's good manners.

Caitlyn got up from the table and kissed the top of Henry's head. "I'll get those pancakes going."

Over the next twenty minutes, she kept busy cooking Henry's breakfast, but her thoughts were on her date with Logan. Wait a minute—this wasn't a date. It was simply planning her son's surprise birthday party. Nothing more. She bit her lower lip and twisted a strand of hair. But if it was only a planning session, why was she so worried about choosing the right outfit to wear?

An hour later, Caitlyn's stomach twisted when she stepped inside the Hummingbird Café. Before leaving Luke's house, she'd spent ten minutes staring at her outfits hanging in the closet. She finally decided on her pink sundress paired with white wedged-sole sandals. Caitlyn wasn't sure why, but she wanted to look especially nice for her meeting with Logan. Who was she kidding? She knew why.

Caitlyn ignored her rapid pulse and panned her eyes around the crowd enjoying an early lunch. The aroma of sweet onions and steak teased her senses. Having skipped breakfast with Henry, her stomach protested in rumbling response.

The sound of a chair screeching across the walnut wood-plank flooring drew Caitlyn's attention to the far corner of the restaurant. She spotted Logan standing. Her palms moistened when she noticed he was holding a cluster of white and pink forget-me-nots. Feeling as though her feet weren't touching the floor, she floated closer to his table.

With his head slightly tilted, Logan offered her the flowers.

"These are gorgeous. I rarely see them in other colors besides blue." Caitlyn accepted the gift. "Thank you." Her voice shook as their eyes connected.

Logan nodded, his lips parted. "They match your dress." He did a quick once-over of her outfit and his cheeks blushed with color. "You look beautiful."

"Thank you," Caitlyn stuttered. "I can't remember the last time I got dressed for a da—"

Logan stared down into her eyes. "It's okay. You can call it a date." Logan smiled and pulled out the chair directly across from where he'd sat earlier.

Caitlyn's face felt hot as bacon grease in a sizzling skillet. How could she have called it exactly what it wasn't? But if it wasn't a date, why couldn't she stop thinking about what it would be like if Logan kissed her? Caitlyn settled into her chair before her legs gave in from under her. Logan followed her lead. "I'm sorry. I shouldn't have said that."

Logan leaned in. "You didn't. I did. And to be completely honest, it felt great to say it." His eyes twinkled.

What was happening? So Logan thought it was a date, too? Had they both concluded this was indeed a date? She paused and recalled her earlier actions. Preparing for her meeting with Logan, she'd carefully applied her makeup and had taken extra time picking out the outfit she would wear. Her body temperature rose at the realization that she was on her first date since the breakup with Jeffrey. Logan was right. Calling it a date felt great.

An hour after Logan first pulled out the chair for Caitlyn and the two admitted they were on a date, the atmosphere turned playful. Over lunch and copious amounts of sweet tea, they each shared stories about their pasts.

Time was like a horse out of the starting gate. Logan

wanted the afternoon to go on forever. He wanted to learn everything possible about Caitlyn Calloway. What were her dreams? Did she want more children? But the guise of their so-called meeting had to be addressed. Henry's party. Truth be told, Logan already had everything under control—almost everything. The one thing that did matter was discussing his gift to Henry. He had to find the perfect segue. Logan agreed with Cody. Springing the dog on Caitlyn at the party was definitely a way to backfire his entire plan.

"I suppose we should do a little party planning." Caitlyn dabbed her lips with the cloth napkin.

How did she do that? It was as though she'd read his mind. Had Caitlyn also read the part where he wondered what it would be like to kiss her? "You're right." Logan watched Caitlyn remove the ubiquitous journal from her bag. "I wondered when that would make an appearance," Logan laughed.

"I couldn't sleep last night, so I made a list of things I need to pick up at Garrison's. If they don't have some items, I'll make a trip to Denver since I need to do a little clothes shopping."

Logan's ears perked up at the mention of Caitlyn traveling to Denver. "Maybe we could go together."

"You're already doing enough. Henry and I can go."

Logan took in a couple of deep breaths. "Really, it's not a problem at all." It was a problem if he couldn't take her. The idea of Caitlyn and Henry going alone to Denver didn't sit well with him. But if he told her the reason, she might think he was acting irrational. Denver was a safe city, but after what had happened to Melody, Logan doubted whether any city was safe. As silly as it sounded, if Logan had his way, everyone he loved would stay in the safe little town of Bluebell and never leave.

"Why don't we go over the list I made first and go from there?" Caitlyn suggested.

Caitlyn opened the journal. They both leaned in at the same time and their heads bumped.

"Sorry," they said in unison, laughing.

Logan enjoyed the proximity to Caitlyn. He could smell her shampoo. It reminded him of the honeysuckle back in Virginia.

"The good news is I've already taken care of most of what you covered on your list." Logan continued to scan the numerical listing, running his finger down the page.

Caitlyn took a pen from her bag and double-checked the list. "So you have already sent out the invitations and ordered the cake?"

Logan nodded. "Yes, ma'am, that's all done. I didn't think it would be fair for me to offer to throw a party for Henry at my house and then dump all the preparations on you."

"Maybe not, but he is my son. I can't expect you to do all the work." Caitlyn pulled away, creating a little distance between them.

"I'll be honest. I sent a few text messages, but once I told Nellie to spread the word, the entire town was aware of the party in under an hour." Logan grinned. "Besides, I've left you with the most important job that didn't make your list."

Caitlyn gazed down at the page before looking back up at Logan. She tapped her finger against her lower lip. "I'm afraid to ask what that might be."

"While preparing for the party, it's imperative you keep it a secret from Henry. You've probably already realized that Bluebell is a town where everyone seems to know what's going on. Of course, some, who shall remain nameless, make a point of knowing more about their neighbor's private life than others." Logan smirked.

Caitlyn chuckled. "I'll do my best to keep Henry in the dark. It won't be easy, though. He doesn't seem to miss a thing. I've made a point of not leaving my journal lying around, even though he's never showed much interest in what I write."

"I think as long as we do our communications about the party through text messages, we should be okay. Since I'm taking care of purchasing all the party supplies, you don't have to worry about Henry finding anything around Luke's house."

"I wanted to discuss that with you." Caitlyn leaned back in her chair. "Can you keep a tally of all of your expenses for the party so I can reimburse you?"

Logan had expected some pushback from Caitlyn. "No way. This party was my idea, so I am paying for everything. Henry is a great kid, and he deserves a special day."

Tears sprung from Caitlyn's eyes. She quickly grabbed her napkin.

"What's wrong? Why are you crying?" Logan placed his hand on Caitlyn's arm.

"I'm sorry. This is embarrassing." She wiped her face with the napkin. "It's just—I can't tell you what this means to me. Henry has so many challenges in his life. It's nice to know someone else cares."

"There are many people in this town who care for Henry—and for you. Maybe you don't realize it, but it's true," Logan told her.

Caitlyn nodded her head slowly. "I'm starting to see that, but my concern is Henry's growing attachment to you and this community. It's going to be difficult for him when it's time to leave."

"What about you?" Logan kept his eyes focused on Caitlyn. "Do you have any feelings about leaving?"

Caitlyn slowly shook her head. "I don't have any other option."

"Can I get you both some more sweet tea?" The young waitress holding a pitcher of tea slipped up to the edge of the table, catching them off guard.

Logan watched as Caitlyn's shoulders relax in relief at the opportunity to change the subject.

"I'd love a refill." She pushed her glass toward the pitcher.

"Same here," Logan responded.

The waitress refilled the glasses and moved to another table.

Logan glanced at his watch. He was running out of time. There was no easy way to bring up the subject of Cooper, other than to just say it. "There's something else that's not on your list that I need to talk with you about."

Caitlyn took a sip of her tea. "Let me start a new page." She placed her finger on the paper, but Logan touched her hand so she couldn't turn the page.

"No, this doesn't need to be written. It's about my gift to Henry."

Caitlyn's eyebrow squished together. "But the party is your present. It's the most special gift he'll receive."

"Not necessarily. There's something I can give to Henry and to you that's far greater than any party I can host. I know you said no when I mentioned it before, but I hope once you hear me out, you'll change your mind."

Caitlyn picked at the corner of her journal. "I assume you're referring to the seizure dog?"

Logan nodded. "Yes, but there's something I need to ask you. I hope the question won't offend you, but I have to know. Is the only reason you said no to Henry having a service dog because of financial reasons?"

Caitlyn's expression went blank, and she turned away.

Logan had his answer. He had assumed that was why. The subject of money was never easy to discuss, but he had to try. Logan reached and took her hand. "You can talk to me. There's nothing to be ashamed of. I'm your friend and I'd like to help you."

Caitlyn faced him again. She hesitated for a moment before straightening her shoulders. "I'm broke." She picked up her glass and drained the last of the tea. "That's the reason I have to sell Last Dollar, because I'm down to my last dollar." She half laughed. "That's a bit of an exaggeration, but I'm pretty close. Despite the health coverage I have for Henry, since his diagnosis, the medical bills have nearly sent me into bankruptcy. I'm behind on my rent. Our landlord has been patient with me, but if I don't catch up soon, Henry and I are going to lose our home."

Logan's stomach turned. It was worse than he'd imagined. "I can help you."

Caitlyn wiped her eyes. "You've done so much already. You and everyone in this town have helped me get the house ready to put on the market. But the financial situation is my problem and I have to fix it."

Logan understood Caitlyn's determination to maintain her independence. "I admire you for everything you're doing to give Henry the best life, but you don't have to do it on your own. A service dog could benefit him and possibly help to reduce some of your unexpected medical bills, particularly with the emergency room visits."

"I'll be honest with you. I've researched those benefits, so I know what you say is true. But I've also researched the cost involved in training a dog to help someone like Henry. There's just no way I could afford that right now."

"But that's where you're wrong." Logan leaned closer to Caitlyn. "With God, all things are possible."

For the next fifteen minutes, Logan provided Caitlyn with the backstory on Cooper, and how the dog had become available. He had to give her credit. Caitlyn listened intently and even scribbled down a few notes in her journal.

"So, Cooper has had the training to work as a seizure dog?" Caitlyn asked.

Logan nodded. "Yes, pretty much. I've been working with him, but he's as ready as he's going to be to transition to his handler."

Caitlyn sat quietly for a moment.

Logan was aware Caitlyn didn't want to be anyone's charity case. She had a lot of pride, so it was important for him to make things clear. "The organization who initially trained Cooper operates on donations from individuals and corporations. It's their business to train and gift the dogs to people in need of a service dog. So, if you don't take Cooper, someone else will. And that person won't pay anything either."

Caitlyn stared straight ahead, processing the information Logan had provided. Countless emotions moved across Caitlyn's face, but he couldn't get a feel for which direction she was leaning, so he waited patiently for a response.

"When can I meet Cooper?" Caitlyn smiled.

Hope flamed like a lighthouse keeper's oil lamp. Having Caitlyn agree to meet Cooper was the first step in his plan to keep Caitlyn and her son in Bluebell. Of course, having her say yes to his offer to buy Last Dollar was a big jump from saying yes to meeting a service dog. But Logan had faith and a plan. Caitlyn wasn't the only one keeping a to-do list. At the top of Logan's list was convincing Caitlyn to stay in Bluebell.

Chapter Thirteen

"Why are we walking to Mr. Logan's house? Wouldn't it be a lot faster just to drive over there?" Henry inquired.

Caitlyn lost her footing as they climbed the grassy path that connected Luke's home to Logan's property. Following two weeks of party planning, the big day had arrived. She could hardly contain her excitement. When her foot slipped a second time, she clenched her teeth. She should have worn her flat sandals or maybe even tennis shoes, but she'd decided on the wedge-heeled sandals because they looked better with her outfit. She'd wanted to look good for Logan. "It's such a nice day today I thought you'd enjoy a walk. Plus, it's your birthday. I want to spend as much time as possible with you." Caitlyn reached for Henry's hand.

Henry looked up at her. "I guess walking isn't so bad, but since we're doing so much of it, can we go by the pond and check to see if Donald has come back?"

Caitlyn glanced at her watch. The party would start at noon, so most of the guests were probably at Logan's house by now. That was the reason she and Henry were walking instead of driving. Last night, Logan had sent a text suggesting they walk so they could come inside around the back of the property to avoid seeing all the cars parked in the driveway. She knew Henry would be full of questions.

"We don't have time to stop at the pond, maybe later. Mr. Logan is expecting us for lunch. We don't want to keep him waiting."

While they continued the hike, Caitlyn's excitement for Henry's big day grew. Last week, after meeting Cooper, the sweet labradoodle, she could hardly wait for today. The party would surprise Henry, but Logan's gift would be the highlight of the day. Henry had dreamed of having a dog and now, thanks to Logan, that dream would come true.

Several minutes later, Caitlyn crested the top of the hill. The early afternoon sun was warm against her face as she peeled off her yellow cardigan and tossed it over her right arm. The three-quarter-length striped top and jean capris provided more than enough warmth for Caitlyn.

"So where do you think Mr. Logan is going to take me for my birthday lunch?" Henry asked.

"He didn't tell me, so I suppose he wants it to be a surprise."

"I like surprises." Henry skipped down the path.

Caitlyn looked down at the bottom of the hill and spotted Logan stepping out onto the patio. He looked up as though he sensed her presence. Or maybe that was a dream. Her heartbeat quickened. Caitlyn couldn't deny feeling just as excited at the thought of spending more time with Logan as she was for Henry's big day.

Thoughts of Logan had lingered in her heart since their date at the Hummingbird Café. The repairs on Last Dollar were wrapping up, limiting her time with Logan, and leaving an ache in her chest. Only cleaning and detailing remained, which she and Henry could do on their own. How had six weeks passed so quickly?

During their time apart, Logan's words weighed heavy on her heart. *With God, all things are possible.* Upon her arrival in Bluebell, her one goal was a better life for Henry. Selling the property was the only way to provide her with a stable foundation for Henry's future. But time spent with Logan and experiencing small-town living had made her realize what was truly important. The love of family and friends mattered most. Selling Last Dollar wasn't what was best for Henry. Could she somehow keep the house? Maybe sell the land? Would that leave her with enough money to pay her landlord and Henry's medical bills? What would happen to her barrel racing school?

Logan threw up a hand and waved.

Henry ran to Logan and wrapped his arms around Logan's waist. The hug lingered.

Caitlyn closed her eyes. Warmth filled her body while her heart demanded answers. Was there a way she could give Henry his birthday wish to remain in Bluebell?

"Happy birthday, kiddo." Logan was the first to pull away from Henry as Caitlyn stepped onto the patio.

"Thanks! I feel like we've been walking for days," Henry laughed.

"Oh, come on. My house isn't that far." Logan turned to Caitlyn. "What about you?"

Caitlyn looked down at her feet. "I would have been a lot better off if I'd worn tennis shoes."

"But they wouldn't have gone as well with your outfit, right?" Logan smiled. "By the way, you look great."

Logan moved closer and gave Caitlyn a quick hug. She yearned for his touch to linger.

"Let's go inside and get you some water before we head out for lunch." Logan placed his hand on Henry's shoulder and tossed a wink in Caitlyn's direction.

Caitlyn could hardly contain her excitement. Thanks to Logan, this would be a day her son would never forget.

She watched as Henry pushed open the French doors and stepped inside.

"Surprise!" The crowd of partygoers, now like family, cheered. Their hoots and hollers echoed throughout the home.

Henry turned around to face Caitlyn and Logan. "Is this all for me?" His eyes widened in surprise and confusion.

Overwhelmed with emotion, Caitlyn couldn't speak. She followed Logan into the house.

The open space encompassing the family room and kitchen was overflowing with children and adults clapping and cheering. Their faces ignited with affection. A spark of anticipation danced in her chest, knowing that the man she was falling for had orchestrated this party for Henry. "It's all for you, sweetie." Caitlyn moved closer and gave Henry a hug.

Henry's eyes darted from one person to another. "How did they know it was my birthday?" he asked, his voice a mix of confusion and awe.

Caitlyn knelt in front of Henry. She wiped the tears from her eyes. "Mr. Logan arranged this surprise party to celebrate you," she explained, her voice shaking. "They're here to let you know they think you're pretty special."

Henry's face lit with radiance, overcome by all the attention. A large group of children raced to his side, bearing gifts and shouting birthday wishes.

Caitlyn watched with overwhelming gratitude for the love and acceptance that surrounded Henry. The townspeople had welcomed her and Henry with open arms and embraced them as if they were long-lost family. As she watched Henry's face beam with joy, a sense of peace overpowered Caitlyn. Bluebell was where they belonged.

* * *

"Doesn't he look like a lovesick puppy dog?" Jake side-eyed Cody and then reached out and squeezed Logan's shoulder. Since Logan had first spotted Caitlyn coming down the hill, he hadn't taken his eyes off her. His mind swirled with thoughts of hosting future birthday parties for Henry—together, maybe with a couple of their own kids. Earlier, when they'd hugged, he'd sensed something different about her, but he hadn't been able to quite put his finger on it until now. He watched as Caitlyn moved effortlessly through the crowd. She laughed and connected with everyone around her as though this was their home and they were hosting the party together—as husband and wife. Could that be what she wanted, too? Oh, man. His brothers were right. He was falling in love with her. "Come on, guys, someone is going to hear you."

"It's not like everyone in town doesn't already know. Well, everyone but you," Jake said.

Jake was usually right, but this time, he couldn't be more wrong. Logan knew exactly how he felt about Caitlyn. He wanted to build a life with her and Henry. But with her plans still in place to leave Bluebell, he needed to let her know his feelings without threatening her desire to remain self-reliant.

"You can't let her get away. This is your second chance. But you're running out of time," Cody added.

Cody's words rang true. This was exactly what had kept Logan awake at night for the past week. "It's not that easy. She has her reasons for selling the farmhouse and returning to Wyoming." Logan never kept secrets from his brothers. But sharing Caitlyn's financial situation wouldn't be the right thing to do.

"You need to let her know how you feel before it's too

late," Jake said. "There's nothing more I want for you than to have what Olivia and I share."

"Thanks, buddy. I appreciate it."

Logan had witnessed the change in Jake's life when he and Olivia had married. After Jake had lost his first wife, Logan had questioned whether his brother would ever find happiness again. But God had brought Olivia into his life and everything had changed for the better. And now God had done the same for him by orchestrating this reunion between him and Caitlyn.

Logan inhaled a deep breath and expelled it. "I've decided I'm going to put an offer on Caitlyn's childhood home. Maybe if she stays and rents the property from me for a while, it can give us a chance at a future together. I plan to speak with Larry at the bank about getting a loan."

"Oh, man, this is huge." Grinning, Cody slapped Logan on the back.

"You think?" Logan gazed around the room to make sure nobody could overhear their conversation. "Can we keep it down?"

"So when are you going to propose?" Jake asked.

"Hold on a second. I just said I need more time." Logan rubbed the back of his neck. "We haven't even had a first date."

Jake shook his head. "That's not what I heard. Nellie told me that Sally Raphine told her you two were on a date at the Hummingbird Café."

"Yeah, Nellie told me you even gave her forget-me-nots," Cody added.

"Boy, nothing gets past that woman, does it?" Even though Logan and Caitlyn had both thought their planning session at the café was a date, it hadn't been official. Logan wanted to take Caitlyn on a legitimate date. One where he picked her up at the door and presented her with the biggest bouquet of forget-me-nots he could hold in his hands.

"Dating is so overrated," Cody stated.

Jake and Logan laughed.

"I guess that's why you're still single with no prospects." Jake nudged his younger brother. "So, have you told Caitlyn about your plan to buy the property?"

"It's kind of complicated."

"What's complicated? You love her and she loves you," Cody said.

Logan put up a hand. "Whoa, I don't know if she loves me."

"That's not what Nellie says, but whatever. You want her to stay in Bluebell, don't you?" Cody asked.

"Of course I do." But is that what Caitlyn wanted? Was she open to the possibility of a future with him?

"Any idea on when the house goes on the market?" Cody asked.

"Since addressing all the major repairs, she will list it after the Fourth of July."

"The Fourth is a week from today." Cody's eyes widened.

"You don't say." Logan was aware of the ticking clock.

"What about her barrel racing school? Do you think she would give that up?" Jake asked.

"I could never ask her to do that. It means the world to her, but I believe there's a demand here in Bluebell. There's only one facility like hers in Denver, but I recently heard the instructor Mitchell McCain is getting ready to retire."

"That sounds like perfect timing to me," Jake said. "Maybe you should contact him to find out more details on the class sizes and enrollment numbers."

Logan was one step ahead of Jake. "I left him a voice mail yesterday. His greeting said he's out of the office and would return calls on Monday. I'm sure I'll be able to talk with him early next week."

"Caitlyn is sitting on a desirable piece of property. Last year, the Bakers' property had a bidding war the first day it went on the market. Are you prepared for that?" Jake asked.

"The market isn't as hot as it was last year, so I'm not too concerned." Logan was more worried about his loan being denied. He couldn't risk losing Caitlyn and Henry. They both had become an important part of his life. He wasn't ready to let them go.

Jake moved a little closer and spoke softer. "I don't want to be pessimistic, but what if Caitlyn says no to your idea?"

"Believe me. I've had plenty of sleepless nights thinking about that. Caitlyn and I both carry some relationship baggage. It's taken me a long time to get over losing Melody, but I'm ready to take a chance on love again. Caitlyn's last relationship left her pretty jaded. If she has reservations, I'll give her all the time she needs. But I'll do everything in my power to prove how much I love her and Henry."

Cody playfully nudged Logan's arm. "Come on, man. You've got this. Caitlyn is crazy about you."

Jake patted Logan on the back. "Opening your heart to someone is always risky, but it's worth it." He tipped his head and whispered, "You better get over there before some other cowboy tries to swoop in on her."

Logan glanced across the room at Caitlyn. She offered a sweet smile, providing him with the confidence he needed. "I'm not about to let that happen."

Cody grabbed Logan's arm as he took Jake's advice. "One more question. When are you going to give Cooper to Henry?"

"Caitlyn and I thought it was best to do it after the party, once everyone else has gone home." Logan hoped he and

Caitlyn could have a little alone time after Henry went to bed. That was another reason Logan had asked Caitlyn and Henry to walk over to the party, so he could walk them home.

"Make sure you take some photos or a video. I want to see Henry's reaction," Jake said.

"Will do. Thanks for listening. And don't forget to take some food home with you, otherwise I'm going to have leftovers for the next month." Logan turned and headed to Caitlyn, who stood alone, sipping a cup of punch, staring out the French doors that went to the patio.

Logan slipped up behind her and whispered, "It's a million-dollar view, isn't it?"

Caitlyn smoothed her hair. "I was hoping you'd come over and enjoy it with me," she sighed.

Logan's insides vibrated. He wanted nothing more than to enjoy the breathtaking scenery and every other precious moment with Caitlyn for the rest of his life.

"You and your brothers all have fantastic views. I've been spending as much time as I can on Luke's wraparound porch. Hanging out on the swing makes me forget about all of my troubles—at least for a while." She smiled.

Was she spending any of that time thinking about him? Or possibly reconsidering her plan for leaving Bluebell? Logan wasn't sure how much longer he could keep his feelings for her contained. The atmosphere swirled with a sense of possibilities.

"Thank you for today, Logan." Caitlyn turned and touched his arm. "I can't tell you how much this day means to Henry. How much it means to me. You've made Henry the happiest little boy in the state of Colorado."

"He deserves all the happiness in the world." Logan paused for a moment, his gaze unwavering. "You both do."

Caitlyn stood quietly. A tear ran down her cheek.

Logan lifted his thumb to her face and gently wiped away the tear. "This is a day for smiles, not for tears."

"I know." Caitlyn shook her head. "I'm sorry, but I'm just so happy."

"So am I," Logan confided. "I promise you, the best is yet to come."

Caitlyn nodded quickly. "You're right. I can hardly wait to see Henry's face when he meets Cooper."

Logan took Caitlyn's hand. "Let's go somewhere private." He led her outside to the empty patio area. A cool breeze brushed his face as he gently intertwined his fingers with hers. "I'm excited for Henry to meet Cooper, too, but that wasn't exactly what I was referring to when I said the best is yet to come," Logan clarified while his heart pounded in his chest.

Caitlyn looked up. Her eyes shimmered with emotion. "I can't imagine things ever getting any better than they are at this moment."

Logan stepped closer. He tenderly cupped her chin with his hand. His heart pounded with nervous anticipation.

Caitlyn's eyes met his and she leaned in.

Logan softly pressed his mouth against hers. There was no resistance as she fell into his arms. He savored the delicate softness of her lips and the warmth of her breath with the hope the feeling would last forever.

Ever so slightly, the kiss grew in intensity until Caitlyn slowly pulled away and looked up. Her eyes sparkled with a newfound understanding. "I was wrong. This is better."

Chapter Fourteen

Two hours later, after the last guests had said their goodbyes, Logan's house was finally empty. While Henry played outside on the patio, Caitlyn was enjoying the lingering effects of Logan's lips against her own. She stood at the kitchen sink and mindlessly washed the dishes, reliving how safe she felt in his arms. The kiss was something she'd hoped for, yet it had caught her totally by surprise. But that was Logan—a man full of surprises.

"What are you doing over there?" Logan approached, his earlier smile replaced with a frown. "I won't have the mother of the guest of honor washing dishes." He tugged the dishtowel from Caitlyn's hand.

"It's the least I can do after the spectacular party you threw for Henry. You shouldn't have to clean up by yourself." Caitlyn scanned her surroundings. "Look at the place. It's a mess."

"If I was concerned about it, I would have taken Nellie up on her offer to clean up with some ladies from church. Don't worry about any of that now. I can take care of it later. It's time to introduce Henry to Cooper." Logan took Caitlyn's hand and guided her to the patio doors. "You go ahead outside and hang with Henry while I get Cooper from the kennel and bring him around."

Caitlyn jumped up and down, clapping her hands.

"Shh…you don't want to spoil the surprise," Logan laughed.

Caitlyn dropped her hands to her sides. "I'm sorry. I can't wait to see his reaction. It means the world to me you've done this for Henry."

"Be patient. You won't have to wait much longer. Go ahead outside with him, but don't say anything about the dog."

Caitlyn watched Logan head to the front door. She did as he instructed and stepped out onto the patio. Logan's selflessness and kindness overwhelmed her. Cooper would change Henry's life. She took a deep breath to steady her emotions.

Henry wasn't aware Caitlyn had joined him on the patio, so she remained quiet, watching him play. Her eyes watered in anticipation. This would be a moment that belonged to Henry.

Seconds later, the sounds of a barking dog caused Henry to jerk his attention away from the toy car. Henry's eyes popped wide open. He dropped to the ground when he spotted Cooper running toward him. The dog covered Henry's face with sloppy licks. "Where did you come from?" Henry giggled as Cooper rolled over onto his back with his legs up in the air.

Caitlyn walked closer, but stopped when Logan stepped onto the patio.

"Is this one of the new dogs you're training?" Henry asked. "I think he likes me."

Logan knelt in front of Henry and the dog. "You might be right. I've never seen him this excited to meet someone."

"What's his name?" Henry rubbed Cooper's belly while the dog licked his hand.

"His name is Cooper."

"That's a cool name. Is he going to help be somebody's eyes like Sophie?"

"Actually, he's trained to work as a seizure dog."

Caitlyn watched for Henry's reaction.

Henry pulled his hand from Cooper and looked up at Logan. "Like my seizures?"

Logan nodded. "Exactly like yours."

Henry bit on his lower lip. "That's good. I hope the dog helps the person."

Caitlyn fought back her tears.

"Well, I guess you can let me know." Logan looked over at Caitlyn and motioned her to come over.

Caitlyn's legs wobbled as she moved closer. The reality of what was about to happen settled in. Henry was about to receive a gift that could change his life forever, all thanks to Logan.

"What do you mean?" Henry asked.

"Do you want to tell him?" Logan asked Caitlyn.

She forced down the lump that had formed in her throat. "No, I think you should be the one."

Logan nodded. "Cooper is your dog."

Henry's face squished. "I don't understand."

Logan sat beside Henry on the concrete. "Cooper belongs to you now. He's going to help you manage your seizures."

"How can he do that?" Henry asked.

"Cooper can detect the signs of an oncoming seizure," Logan explained. "He has a remarkable ability to sense changes in your body, even before you realize something is happening."

Henry's brow furrowed. "How can he do that before I know?"

"It's hard to understand, but dogs have an incredible

sense of smell. Cooper can detect the unique scent your body releases when a seizure is about to happen. When he recognizes the scent, he'll do everything in his power to alert you and those around you to make sure you're safe."

Henry's eyes widened with realization. "For real?"

"Yes, indeed. Cooper will be right by your side. When he senses a seizure, he might bark, paw at you, or even run to get help. He'll do whatever he can to make sure you're protected and taken care of."

"That's so cool." Henry turned to Caitlyn. "Did you hear that, Mom?"

Caitlyn shook her head. "I did. That's pretty amazing." Caitlyn took notice of the sense of relief that washed over Henry's face as he absorbed the information. The fear of seizures had always lingered in the back of his mind, but now, with Cooper by his side, he felt a newfound sense of security.

"But Cooper is more than just your seizure dog. He'll be your loyal companion. He's here to provide you with unconditional love and support. When you're feeling down or lonely, he'll be there to snuggle with you, play with you, and make you smile. He's your best friend, always ready to listen and comfort you."

Henry's eyes glistened with tears of joy. "I love him already." He leaned over, wrapped his arms around Cooper's neck, and buried his face into the dog's coat. "He even smells good!"

Logan pulled the leather leash from his back pocket and secured it to Cooper's collar. He passed the leash to Henry's hand.

Henry turned his attention from Logan to Caitlyn. "So, I can really keep him?"

"Yes, sweetie. Cooper belongs to you."

"But you said I couldn't have a dog."

Logan looked at Caitlyn and winked. Her pulse quickened.

"Mr. Logan changed my mind."

Henry jumped to his feet and threw his arms around Logan's neck. "Thank you! You've made this birthday the best one ever. I can't believe I have a dog of my own!"

Tears streamed down Caitlyn's cheeks as she watched the love her son had for Logan. She couldn't deny the positive impact Logan had made on Henry's life by giving him a trained seizure dog. Yet, beneath the surface of her gratitude, there was a pang of worry. She'd ignored calls from the landlord. To buy some time, she'd sent him a text message that she'd have his money soon. But would that mean leaving Bluebell? Thoughts of separating Henry from Logan weighed heavily on her heart. But an even greater weight was the thought of leaving the man she loved.

"I didn't know you were such a talented cupcake baker." Logan playfully nudged Cody while placing the first tray of patriotic cupcakes decorated with red, white and blue frosting on the table.

Cody slipped his hands into the back pockets of his jeans, pleased with himself. "They look pretty good, don't they? I saw them in a magazine."

"Wait until you try some of my homemade lemonade," Jake chimed in. "I was up past midnight squeezing the lemons."

Logan laughed at his brothers and took in his surroundings. The prediction of a July Fourth washout had never materialized. The afternoon sky was void of clouds, allowing the warm summer sun to fill the town square, now a bustling scene of activity.

Everything had come together, not only with the holiday celebration, but with Logan's plan. He'd invited Caitlyn and Henry to a picnic lunch with him today, since burgers and hotdogs weren't being served until later in the day. Caitlyn had said yes and even offered to bring the food. When the time was right, he wanted to share his intentions with Caitlyn about her property. Once he heard from the bank, he planned to put in an offer on the farmhouse and the land, to give them time to explore a future together.

The kiss they had shared the day of Henry's birthday party had transformed their friendship into something more. Logan felt it, yet Caitlyn still planned to return to Wyoming.

"So have you convinced Caitlyn to stay in Bluebell?" Cody asked, draping a red-, white- and blue-checked tablecloth over a third table.

The bank had called him on Wednesday, requesting more documentation for the loan. He'd also received an update from his attorney that the home would go into the multiple listing database. "I'm going to tell her today I plan to put in an offer after I receive the loan approval. She'll list the property on Monday."

"We better change the subject. Here comes Nellie and her posse," Jake warned, and busied himself setting out liters of soda and paper cups.

The cheerful chatter of the ladies from the church grew. They approached the tables, carrying trays covered with tinfoil.

Nellie made a beeline for Logan. "You and your brothers have done a wonderful job setting everything up. Hank will be here with the flags and several banners any minute."

"We'll be ready," Logan assured Nellie.

"Has Caitlyn arrived?" Nellie scanned the grassy area

where the band was setting up for the concert later this afternoon.

Jake cleared his throat and threw an eye roll in Logan's direction.

"I haven't seen her, but I'm sure she and Henry will come," Logan said.

Nellie waved her hand in the air. "Of course they will. Did you know her house goes on the market on Monday?"

"Yes, I heard something about that."

"I stopped by the farmhouse yesterday to see if Caitlyn needed any help cleaning." Nellie pinched the skin on her throat. "You better hurry and propose or that girl will be long gone back to Wyoming. Today would be the perfect day. You know, Nelson proposed to Thelma during the town's July Fourth celebration. I also have a couple of friends whose grandchildren got engaged here. Proposing marriage during the fireworks is quite romantic, don't you think?"

Jiminy crickets. Nellie's mind never stopped working.

"You know she's in love with you, don't you?"

What? Wait. Had Caitlyn said something to Nellie or was the woman simply sharing her opinion? Either way, Logan was desperate and running out of time, so he couldn't ignore her comment. "Did she tell you that?"

Nellie quickly covered her mouth. "Oh, mercy. I wasn't supposed to say anything." She glanced over her shoulder and stepped closer. "Promise you won't let her know I said something."

Logan put up his hand. "I promise." He rolled his shoulders, waiting for an answer.

"The poor girl is smitten with you. She told me she'd like to stay in Bluebell, but she has some financial reasons that make it impossible. That's why she needs to sell the house." Nellie turned to the sound of a dog's bark. "Oh, goodness, here comes Caitlyn and Henry now. Please don't mention our conversation."

Nellie scurried off in the opposite direction of Caitlyn. Her face flushed in red.

Caitlyn wants to stay in Bluebell. Why hadn't she told him?

"Hi, Mr. Logan! Happy Fourth of July!" Cooper pulled Henry to Logan's side.

"Same to you, buddy. Hey, Coop. Are you behaving?" Logan reached down and patted the dog's head.

"Cooper has been great. Even Mom said she's never seen a dog that acts this behaved," Henry huffed, trying to catch his breath. "There's Kyle and Kayla! I'm going to introduce Cooper to them." Henry took off running toward the cotton candy kiosk.

"Don't go off too far, Henry!" Caitlyn called out.

Logan spun on his heal when he heard Caitlyn. Smiling, he struggled with the emotions swirling inside him. Nellie's news had caught him off guard. He'd sensed Caitlyn might have feelings for him, but he hadn't known she'd changed her mind about leaving Bluebell. His heart raced and his mind couldn't keep up with his thoughts. There was a part of him that wanted to drop on one knee and propose this second, but he needed to stick with his plan.

"Good afternoon." Caitlyn approach, smiling and carrying a large basket.

He caught a whiff of her honeysuckle shampoo It sparked a memory of their first kiss. Dressed in faded jeans and a red-and-white peasant blouse, Caitlyn had pinned her hair up, revealing the slim arc of her neck. Her appearance wasn't helping to calm Logan's pulse. She looked more gorgeous than ever.

Logan took a quick peek inside the basket.

Caitlyn snapped it closed and playfully tapped his hand. "That's our lunch for later."

Logan jerked his hand away. "Yum…it sure smells a lot like my mother's crispy-fried chicken."

"That's because it's her recipe. Nellie gave it to me when she stopped by yesterday. Henry and I enjoyed it so much when you made it for us, I thought I'd return your generosity," she confided, her eyes shining.

Logan wondered if Nellie had passed along the fried chicken recipe before or after Caitlyn had confessed her love for Logan. A soft chuckle escaped his lips.

"What's so funny?" Caitlyn asked.

"It's nothing. I'm just hungry, that's all." Logan glanced at his watch. "If you two are ready to eat, I can finish up here and meet you and Henry at one of the picnic tables at the park in a few minutes."

"It's a date." Caitlyn winked. "I'll get Henry and we'll grab a table." She turned on her heel and went to tell Henry.

"Can Cooper and I go play cornhole with Kyle, Kayla and Mr. Jake until the fireworks start?" Henry downed the last of his soda and jumped up from the picnic table.

"Okay, but make sure you stay with them until I come to get you," Caitlyn instructed.

Logan was happy to see that Cooper had helped to ease Caitlyn's mind, allowing Henry to have more freedom to be a kid. He took the last bite of the crispy-fried chicken. The flavors mingled on his tongue. "Don't worry about Henry. Jake and Olivia can keep an eye on him. We can go watch the fireworks with them later."

Caitlyn nodded and watched Henry run off with Cooper.

"Your chicken turned out perfect. My mother would be

proud." Logan got up from his place across from Caitlyn and rounded the table to sit beside her.

"I'm happy you enjoyed it." She smiled.

"If you cooked a brown paper bag, I'd probably enjoy it." Logan's shoulder bumped hers as he sidled closer to her.

Caitlyn laughed.

Logan took a deep breath and turned to face Caitlyn. "I have something important I'd like to talk with you about."

Caitlyn's expression turned solemn. "What's wrong? This sounds serious."

After days of rehearsing what he wanted to say, Logan decided not to beat around the bush. He took Caitlyn's hand. "I've been thinking. I want you and Henry to stay in Colorado, so we can build a future together."

A mix of surprise and confusion flickered in Caitlyn's eyes. "But I need to sell the property to pay off my debt. I thought you understood."

"I understand. That's why I want to purchase the house so you and Henry can remain in Bluebell. You can rent back from me. It can give us time to see where this is headed." Logan looked down when Caitlyn pulled her hand away.

"I can't expect you to take care of my financial problems. You and the rest of the town have already done more than enough to help me get in a position to sell the house."

Logan brought his hand back to hers, and their eyes connected. "You would still have your independence and be in the position to pay off your debt. It's no different from you selling to a stranger, except if I buy the house, you can rent from me."

"You want to be my landlord? Even knowing what a risk I am?"

"What can I say? I like to take risks." He shrugged. "Besides, we both benefit. I get rental income and you can stay in Bluebell like you want."

"How did you know I changed my mind?"

"Take a guess."

"Nellie. That woman couldn't keep a secret if her life depended on it." Caitlyn shook her head.

"You got that right."

Caitlyn's eyes softened. "But my barrel racing school and all of my students are in Wyoming. How could I possibly move everything to Bluebell?"

"I've been doing research. We can not only move your school to the Last Dollar property, but we can expand it because there is a need. The only school like yours is in Denver and it's closing because the owner, Mitchell McCain, plans to retire. I've already been in contact with him. He's offered to work with us." Logan placed his hand under Caitlyn's chin. "We'll make it work together. We only need more time."

A glimmer of hope filled Caitlyn's eyes. "Are you sure this is what you want?"

Logan nodded slowly. "I want you and Henry here in Bluebell. If given the opportunity, I want us to have a chance at happiness."

"You've already made me happy, Logan," Caitlyn whispered. "More than you'll ever know."

Logan placed his hands on Caitlyn's cheeks, leaned in, and kissed her. But this time, Caitlyn didn't pull away. Instead, they remained in each other's arms until the first fireworks of the evening ignited the sky.

Chapter Fifteen

"I could get used to this." Caitlyn sipped on a glass of iced tea and settled back on the cushioned lounge chair. A chorus of crickets filled the property while an aroma of steak sizzling on the grill filled the air. She leaned her head against the soft cushion. The children were inside munching on hamburgers and hotdogs with Nellie, who had volunteered to babysit for the evening.

"Once you and Henry are permanent residents, we can do this all the time." Logan turned to Jake, who stood flipping the meat to ensure it cooked evenly. "Jake and Olivia love to host cookouts in Jake's overly expensive outdoor kitchen. Isn't that right, big brother?" Logan smirked at Jake.

Since Logan had shared his plans to purchase Last Dollar, her feet hadn't hit the ground. Moments like this evening reminded Caitlyn of the potential for a beautiful future with Logan. The warmth and acceptance she and Henry found within Logan's family and the entire community of Bluebell had left her heart full.

Olivia sat down in the empty chair beside Caitlyn's. A sense of excitement filled her eyes. "It's true. Jake and I were just saying once you're settled in Bluebell, we can do this more often. Not only is it great for us to hang out with other couples, but the kids love to have their cousins—" Olivia flushed.

Logan laughed at Olivia. "It's okay to call Henry a cousin, Liv. Right now, he might not be legally in the family, but if I have my way and this beautiful woman agrees to be my wife one day, Henry will be a legit cousin." Logan winked at Caitlyn.

"Yeah, Luke and his family don't make it back to Colorado as much as we'd like. And, of course, we're still waiting for Cody to settle down and start having a family. But by that time, Kayla, Kyle and Maddie might be off to college," Jake joked. "Okay, let's eat."

Olivia was the perfect hostess, directing Caitlyn and Logan to the outdoor table with citron candles and a large vase of forget-me-nots in the middle. Jake ferried the steaks from the grill on a platter and served everyone before taking one himself.

Logan cut into his meat and took a bite. "The steak is perfect."

"I agree," Caitlyn said after trying a taste.

"Well done, hon." Olivia patted Jake on the back.

"Thanks. I'm glad you like it." Jake placed his napkin on his lap and turned to Caitlyn. "How's everything going with the offers on your property? Any updates from the agent?"

Caitlyn had prayed Logan's loan approval would happen sooner rather than later. "There's been one offer so far, but it was way below my asking price."

"Don't worry, it will all work out." Logan spoke with a reassuring smile. "Speaking of, I forgot to tell you, Mitchell McCain sent over a list of his students who are interested in signing up for your school."

Caitlyn's stomach squeezed. "Isn't that a little premature? I haven't officially moved the school to Colorado. What if something happens?"

Logan leaned over and kissed Caitlyn's cheek. "Nothing is going to happen. Mitchell has explained the situation to everyone, so they understand. Promise me you'll quit worrying about every little thing."

"What will happen to your existing students in Wyoming?" Olivia asked.

"Fortunately, before I came to Bluebell, my class of six graduated. We had the ceremony a week before I left town. My next class doesn't start until the fall. So far only two students have registered. I've contacted the parents and explained my circumstances. They were very understanding especially after I gave them the name of another instructor close to my school."

"See, everything will work out fine. So you don't need to go home and start scribbling in that journal of yours." Logan shrugged and took a bite of his corn on the cob.

After everyone had finished their meal, Olivia and Nellie rounded up the children to come outside for ice cream. Giggles and laughter, along with the occasional bark of a dog, filled the air. The kids gathered around the picnic table with dripping cones in their hands, their eyes wide with excitement.

Caitlyn watched Henry interacting with the kids and her heart warmed. If everything went as planned, this could be Henry's forever home, thanks to Logan.

Moments later, Caitlyn heard an odd sound overhead. She looked up and blinked in disbelief as she watched a familiar figure swoop into the backyard. It was Donald. She couldn't believe her eyes.

"Mom! Look!"

Henry was the first of the children to spot the duck.

His eyes widened with surprise and joy. "It's Donald! She came back because she knows I'm not leaving Bluebell!"

A wave of relief washed over Caitlyn. Even with Cooper in the picture, Henry had worried incessantly about Donald since she had gone missing. He'd believed the duck had left because she'd known he and Caitlyn would leave Bluebell and return to Wyoming.

Henry raced to the duck, but Cooper got there first. With all the commotion, Donald got spooked and flew away. Henry turned in tears. "She's gone again."

Logan jogged over to Henry and knelt in front of him. "Don't worry. Donald just got scared by all the excitement. I think she popped in to let you know she's back. I'm sure she's flown back to the pond."

"Really? You think so?" Henry wiped his eyes.

"Positive." Logan took Henry's hand. "If it's okay with your mom, we can walk over there and look. It won't be dark for a while."

Henry spun around to Caitlyn. "Can we?"

"Of course you can. I'll stay here and help Olivia clean up."

"We want to go, too!" Kayla and Kyle chimed in.

"Jake, you take the kids. They need to walk some of that sugar out of their system." Olivia picked up Maddie. "I'll get this sleepyhead ready for bed."

Nellie moved across the patio and opened her arms. "Let me take care of this little one. I'll get her bathed and into her jammies."

"Thanks, Nellie."

"Okay, kids. Are you ready to go find Donald?" Logan asked.

"Yes!" The children cheered and Cooper responded with a bark.

Caitlyn watched Henry take Logan's hand, and they headed out. Logan seemed sure Donald would be at the pond. For Henry's sake, she hoped he was right.

As Caitlyn grabbed a couple of plates from the table, her cell phone vibrated in the back pocket of her jeans. She set the dishware back down, removed the device, and tapped the screen.

Urgent. Check your email. These letters came in the mail today. Susan

Before leaving for Colorado, she'd asked her neighbor, Susan, to collect the mail. She'd given her permission to open anything that didn't appear to be junk. "I've got a work-related email I have to take care of. I'll be inside in a minute to help you with the dishes," Caitlyn called out to Olivia.

"Take your time," Olivia responded and stepped inside.

Caitlyn opened the email and her legs grew weak. She dropped into the nearby chair. Susan had forwarded a scanned letter from the hospital. They'd threatened legal action if Caitlyn didn't pay the past-due bills in full. Susan had also sent a scanned letter from an attorney representing her landlord. He demanded all back rent to be paid or the eviction process would begin.

The following morning as Henry slept, Caitlyn paced Luke's kitchen floor drinking her third cup of coffee. Unable to sleep, Caitlyn had left her bed at dawn. For the next hour, she'd sat on the front porch and prayed for guidance. Later, she'd returned to the kitchen table, opened her laptop and composed a response to Susan's email.

Yesterday, after Logan, Jake and the kids had returned from the pond, and confirmed Donald was back on the water, Caitlyn and Henry had abruptly left Jake and Olivia's house. She'd blamed the onset of a headache, which had actually hit her after reading the unexpected email from her neighbor. Logan had sensed she was upset and questioned her, but she'd insisted it was just the headache. Caitlyn had decided not to bring up the impeding legal action against her. This was her problem to deal with.

Caitlyn settled back in front of her laptop to clean out her mailbox. Apart from the email Susan had sent yesterday, Caitlyn had neglected to check her emails since last Thursday. Most people texted these days, anyway. She scrolled through the messages, deleting one week of junk mail that had somehow made it into her box. Her finger moved from the delete key when she spotted an email from her real estate agent. He explained he'd had to leave town unexpectedly for a family emergency, but wanted to share the written offer he'd received on Last Dollar.

Logan still hadn't heard from the bank. Why was it taking so long? Maybe that's the way things operated in a small town. Until they approved him, Caitlyn had to consider all offers, so she opened the correspondence from her agent.

Caitlyn's heart pounded in her chest. If she hadn't already consumed a pot of coffee this morning, she would have thought she was dreaming when she read the size of the offer. Her agent explained that a developer wanted the house and all the property to open a dude ranch resort.

Was this the answer to her prayers? With all the money on the table, she could pay everyone in full and have a substantial nest egg in savings. She'd have to walk away from everything—everybody. An opportunity to be debt free was something she'd never dreamed could happen. At what expense? To fulfill Henry's desire to grow up in Bluebell?

A future with Logan? What about the land Logan needed to move forward with his rescue organization?

Caitlyn closed her laptop without responding to her agent. She wrapped her arms around her stomach and leaned forward. She'd wait until Logan got his loan approved and made his offer before she declined the developer's offer.

Early Saturday evening, laughter and lively chatter filled the church social hall. The annual pancake supper was in full swing. The aroma of sweet syrup and coffee filled the air along with the sounds of utensils clicking against plates.

Logan leaned back in his chair and scanned the long table of smiling faces. A sense of contentment filled him. Being here with Caitlyn by his side, Henry, and his family gave him a glimpse into his future.

"Any word on your loan?" Jake leaned across the table.

Logan shook his head. "Nothing yet."

"You'll hear something soon." Jake stood. "I'm going back for seconds."

Logan couldn't shake the feeling that maybe the delay in hearing about his loan troubled Caitlyn. Since the cookout at Jake and Olivia's house when she'd developed the sudden headache, Caitlyn hadn't been herself. He couldn't quite put his finger on it, but she seemed preoccupied. Had she changed her mind?

Suddenly, a million scenarios played through his mind. He needed to know. "Let's go outside for some fresh air," Logan suggested.

Outside the church, Logan took Caitlyn's hand and headed toward the gazebo. They took a seat on the wood bench.

"This is nice, isn't it?" Logan broke the silence. "There should be a brilliant sunset this evening."

"It's beautiful." Caitlyn shivered.

"Are you cold?" Logan extended his arm over Caitlyn's shoulder and pulled her close.

"No, just a chill. I'm fine."

The worry he saw in Caitlyn's eyes told him otherwise. Anticipation built in his chest. He needed to know what was bothering her. "Have you changed your mind about staying in Bluebell?"

"Of course not." Caitlyn squirmed in the seat. "Why would you think that?"

"You've seemed distant the last several days. I thought maybe you'd reconsidered." Logan bit his lower lip.

Caitlyn's hands trembled in her lap. "The last thing I want to do is to get you involved in my financial issues, but I can't keep this to myself any longer."

Logan rubbed her back. "Sweetie, you can tell me. No matter what's bothering you, I'm here for you."

"The hospital is suing me for the medical bills I owe for Henry's treatment." Caitlyn's voice quivered. "They want their payment—like, yesterday."

"I know this is upsetting for you, but everything will work out," Logan said, trying to shut the door on the doubt attempting to creep into his mind.

"It's not only that…my landlord is suing me for the past-due rental income. I'm being overwhelmed by these lawsuits. I don't know how to handle it all."

Caitlyn's phone chirped. She fumbled with her crossover bag. "I'm sorry. I need to make sure that text isn't from my landlord."

"No, go right ahead." Logan looked away while Caitlyn read her message. He focused his eyes on a pair of male and female cardinals perched on the nearby ornamental pear tree bursting with white blooms.

Caitlyn slid her phone inside her bag and released a heavy sigh.

"Is everything all right?" Logan leaned closer.

"That was a message from my real estate agent."

"And?" Logan assumed there had been another offer made on her property.

"This is all so confusing. I wanted to mention it to you, but I needed to pray about it first," Caitlyn said.

"If you don't want to talk about it, that's fine. I understand."

Caitlyn fingered the gold chain around her neck. "I've received another offer." She turned with tears in her eyes. "It's from a developer and it's more than I could have ever imagined."

Logan's chest tightened. Was she going to accept the offer? He swallowed the lump in his throat and reached for her hand. "I want what's best for you and Henry. Whatever you decide, I will support you."

"Thank you for saying that. Of course, it's tempting, but your offer is so much better." Caitlyn squeezed Logan's hand. "I told him I'd have to think about it and get back to him."

Logan's shoulders relaxed. Caitlyn wanted to stay. She wanted a chance at a future together. "Let's go back inside. I could use another stack of pancakes." Logan stood and held her hand tight. He never wanted to let go.

Later that evening, Logan had the windows down on his truck heading up the driveway. The radio played a country song about a lovesick cowboy. He smiled as the singer sang about being head over heels in love. It was a song he could have written himself.

His cell phone rang as he walked inside the kitchen. Logan pulled the device from his pocket. It was Larry from the bank. He'd sent Larry a text message that morning to check on his loan status. An unsettled feeling took hold when he answered the call.

Following a brief conversation, Logan said goodbye. At first, he didn't move or breathe. When his arm dropped to his side, still holding the phone, his first thought was Caitlyn. How would he tell her the bank had declined his loan?

Chapter Sixteen

A week had passed since Caitlyn had reluctantly signed the papers accepting the offer from the real estate developer. After Logan broke the news the bank had declined his loan, she'd had to face the harsh reality. She and Henry had no choice but to return to Wyoming. She tried to explain the situation to Henry, but he didn't fully grasp the implications.

"Sweetie, go put on a clean shirt. We'll be leaving for Kyle and Kayla's house in a few minutes," Caitlyn gently told Henry, hoping to find some way to cheer him up.

Caitlyn had appreciated Olivia's thoughtfulness when she'd called to invite her and Henry to a farewell cookout. Saying goodbye to Logan, his family and Bluebell weighed heavily on her heart.

Henry flopped into the kitchen chair and pouted. Cooper curled up on the floor at his feet, thumping his tail. "I don't really want to go."

Caitlyn's heart ached for Henry. It would be hard for him to leave behind everything he loved in Bluebell. "Don't be silly," she said, trying to sound upbeat. "You always enjoy seeing Kyle and Kayla. We'll have fun. I promise."

"But we're leaving in a couple of days," Henry replied. "I'll probably never see them again, just like I won't ever see Mr. Logan or Donald."

Caitlyn slipped her hands into the back pockets of her jeans and knelt beside Henry, staring into his eyes. "That's not true." She spoke with confidence. "We can come back and visit. Plus, Mr. Logan said he would come to visit us in Wyoming."

Henry's eyes brightened, reflecting a glimmer of hope. "Really?"

"He promised, and you know Mr. Logan doesn't break his promises."

Caitlyn wasn't entirely sure if Logan had made the promise to placate Henry or if he intended to make a trip to Wyoming. But Logan had never given her any reason to doubt his word. He wouldn't make such a promise and not follow through, especially if it would disappoint Henry.

"Now, run along and change your shirt." Caitlyn stood.

"Okay." Henry sprang from the chair and hugged Caitlyn. "Thanks!" He ran from the kitchen. Cooper followed behind on Henry's heels.

Caitlyn's shoulders relaxed. Keeping Henry encouraged the past several days was a challenge. She had a hard enough time keeping her own feelings in check since she wasn't ready to leave Bluebell, and especially Logan.

Her cell alerted her to a new text message from her agent, pulling her from thoughts of a future with Logan. Caitlyn walked to the island, picked up the device and read the text.

Problem with inspection. Call me when you can.

Caitlyn rubbed the back of her neck. With so much going on, the inspection report had slipped her mind. The past few days had been a whirlwind of mixed emotions as she and Henry prepared to head to Wyoming. It had been more difficult for Caitlyn to believe selling the farmhouse and using the proceeds to pay off her debt was the best thing to do for Henry. And was leaving Logan the best for her? But what other choice was there given the pending lawsuits? She stared at the text. With the repairs completed, why did her heart skip a beat when she dialed the agent's number?

Fifteen minutes later, Caitlyn sat at the kitchen table and gazed outside the bay window, watching two rabbits nibble on grass in Luke's backyard. Her mind replayed the conversation with her agent, which had left her reeling. The home inspection had come back yesterday. It revealed termite damage underneath the house. The real estate developer had withdrawn his offer. She placed her hands over her face. Relief and disappointment battled in her mind. Was this part of God's plan? *All things work together for good.* The sickness she felt in the pit of her stomach sure didn't feel so good.

The sound of footsteps entering the kitchen extinguished the loop replaying in her mind.

"What's wrong, Mom? Why are you just sitting there? Don't you need to get ready, too?" Henry's head tilted to one side.

Caitlyn took a deep breath, holding back tears. Henry stood there, wearing a freshly changed polo shirt and looking so grown up. She smiled and opened her arms. "You're right. I do have to get ready, but I need a hug first."

Logan walked up the hill to Jake and Olivia's house and took a deep breath. The late-afternoon sun illuminated a warm glow over the property. After Caitlyn had accepted the investor's offer, a constant ache had gnawed at his chest, knowing this day would come.

Earlier, Logan had prepared himself to say goodbye to

tlyn and Henry, but only until he could figure out a way them to be together again. Deep in his heart, he believed od had brought them together a second time for a reason. nowing this had given him the strength to put a smile on is face and enjoy the cookout with his family and friends.

"Uncle Logan!" Kayla raced across the grass and flung her arms around his waist. "We've been waiting for you to get here so we can play horseshoes. It'll be me and you against Kyle and Uncle Cody."

Logan scooped Kayla up into his arms. "They don't have a chance."

"Hey, brother." Jake approached with a bottle of water in his hand.

"Let me talk to your dad for a minute." Logan put Kayla back on the ground.

"Okay, but don't forget to come to the horseshoe pit." Kayla skipped to the patio.

Jake eyed Logan. "I have to say, you don't look like a man who is about to say goodbye to the woman he loves. I figured you'd be trudging up the hill like you had concrete in your boots."

Logan scanned the patio but didn't see any sign of Caitlyn. "Come on. Isn't there some song about how goodbye doesn't have to mean forever?" Logan reached for his brother's water and took a long pull before passing it back. "You know me. I never give up."

"Yeah, I know. She and Henry aren't here yet, but I guess Caitlyn must have told you already."

Logan scratched his cheek. "Told me what? I haven't talked to her since the day before yesterday."

"That's strange. I thought you would have been the first to know—forget I said anything." Jake waved his hand.

"Forget what? What are you talking about?"

Jake stepped closer. "The investor withdrew his offer on Caitlyn's property."

Logan drew his head back. *Are you kidding me?* Wouldn't he have been the first person Caitlyn would have told? "Are you sure?"

Jake nodded. "Larry told me yesterday while I was at the bank. Apparently, the inspection report showed termites, so the guy walked. He had his eye on another property, so he pulled his offer on Caitlyn's land and jumped on the other."

"Is Larry here? I'd like to talk with him," Logan asked.

"No, he's at the bank working on some big deal, but he said he'd be by later."

"Hi, Henry!" Kyle shouted from the patio.

Logan spun on his heel and spotted Caitlyn and Henry walking down the hill. "I need to find out what's going on. Can you take Henry with you and cover for me at the horseshoe pit?"

"Absolutely." Jake patted Logan on the back.

"Hi!" Henry and Cooper ran ahead of Caitlyn.

"Hey, buddy." Logan winked at Henry and reached down to give Cooper's head a scratch.

Caitlyn avoided eye contact with Logan, but smiled as she approached. "Hey, guys."

Jake stepped forward and gave Caitlyn a quick hug. "It's good to see you. If it's okay, I'd like to take Henry down to the horseshoe pit. The kids have a friendly little match going."

"Cool! Can I?" Henry looked up at his mom.

Caitlyn nodded. "Sure. Have fun."

Logan and Caitlyn stood in silence while Jake led Henry and Cooper down to the games.

"So anything new with you?" Logan hadn't meant to tone irony in his voice, but wasn't he entitled to a little sarcasm?

Caitlyn tucked a strand of hair behind her ear. "I guess you've heard."

"About the termites? Yeah." Logan reached for her hand. "Do you want to take a walk?"

She accepted his hand. "Sure."

They strolled in silence for the first couple of minutes, listening to the children's laughter in the distance. A hawk cried out overhead.

Caitlyn spoke first. "You're right about news spreading like wildfire in a small town. I only found out about the inspection an hour ago. My agent called me. How did you hear?"

"Jake was at the bank yesterday morning. Larry told him." Logan slowed his pace and looked at Caitlyn. "So what now?"

"The place is back on the market. Henry and I will leave as planned."

Logan felt a twinge of regret. If only he'd gotten the loan, Caitlyn and Henry could stay like they'd planned before the developer had come to town. He stopped walking and placed his hands on Caitlyn's face. "Don't worry. Everything will work out." Logan gently kissed her lips and held her close.

Caitlyn pulled back and looked up into his eyes. "Do you promise you'll come visit us in Wyoming?"

Logan ran his hands through her hair and nodded. "I've already been checking flights."

She smiled. "I guess we'd better head back."

"Yeah, Nellie might spread rumors we've run off to elope or something," Logan said, laughing, but he would elope in a heartbeat if Caitlyn agreed.

An hour before sunset, the flames on the grill still flickered while Jake and Olivia made sure there was plenty of food for their guests. Logan found solace, since most of the town had gathered to say goodbye to Caitlyn and Henry. Everyone loved them. The townspeople's somber expressions of the reason for the party mirrored his own. With Jake and Olivia's help, Logan set up a circular bistro table with a candle and an arrangement of forget-me-nots.

"I hope Jake and Olivia are okay with us commandeering their special spot. It's so beautiful here."

"Full confession—it was their idea," Logan said.

Caitlyn's cell phone rang. "I'm sorry. I should have turned the ringer off, but with the house being back on the market, I don't want to miss a call."

"No, by all means, go ahead."

Caitlyn picked up the phone and stepped away from the table.

Logan watched Caitlyn's expression fluctuate between confusion and half smiles. By the time she ended the conversation and returned to the table, she had tears rolling down her cheeks.

Logan jumped from his chair and hurried to her side. "What is it? What's wrong?" He rubbed his hand along her arm.

"That was my agent. An offer came in on my property." Caitlyn wiped her eyes.

"It must be a good one."

Caitlyn studied Logan's face. "It's for the full asking price."

Logan's feelings were mixed. Even though Caitlyn seemed to have made peace with selling her home, a part of him still wanted her to keep it in her family. "That's good—I guess."

"You guess? Is that all you're going to say?" Caitlyn leaned forward and folded her arms across her stomach. "Logan, my agent told me you made the offer."

Logan coughed and took a drink from his glass of water.

"He what? He's mistaken. They denied my loan, remember?"

"I don't understand. Maybe I better call him back." Caitlyn grabbed her phone and hit Redial. "It's gone to voice mail, but the box is full."

Thoughts swirled through Logan's head. Was this some sort of prank? Maybe someone had stolen his identity. There had to be a logical explanation. "Let's go up to the house. Larry is supposed to stop by this evening. Maybe he'll have some answers."

Logan and Caitlyn walked at a steady pace in silence, holding hands. As they crossed the property, Logan noticed the house normally lit up was dark. The crowd that had gathered outside earlier was gone. "Okay, I feel like we're in the twilight zone. What's going on?"

Caitlyn's grip tightened on his hand. "Where is everyone? Where's Henry?" Her pace quickened while she pulled Logan along the grassy path.

Once they reached the patio, Logan flung the French doors open.

"Surprise!" Light filled the area, revealing the entire town packed inside Jake and Olivia's family room and kitchen.

Henry ran to Caitlyn. "Mom, did you hear? We get to stay in Bluebell! Mr. Logan bought our house."

Logan and Caitlyn stood frozen. The room filled with silence as Jake, Cody and Larry approached from across the room.

"What in the world is going on here?" Logan's voice raised as his eyebrows squished together.

Larry laughed. "I guess you guys better tell him." His glances shifted between Jake and Cody.

"We pooled our money and put down the forty percent cash deposit the underwriter required for your loan to be approved," Cody explained. "We started the process after the bank denied your loan, but once the investor came along with his big offer, we figured we couldn't come up with that much cash. It was all Luke's idea. He wished he could be here, but the triplets have the chicken pox."

Larry extended his hand. "Congratulations, son. You're the new owner of Last Dollar."

Cheers and applause broke out as the town stood side by side.

Logan's heart swelled with pride and humility as he realized the impact of his brothers' selfless act of generosity.

Caitlyn looked at Logan's family. Tears pooled in her eyes. "I don't know what to say." She turned. "Logan, I never expected..."

Logan gently took both of her hands into his own. A grin spread from ear to ear. "Nothing is ever impossible when you have God, family and friends by your side. Welcome home."

Epilogue

One year later

"I can't believe our first summer camp starts in less than a week." Caitlyn closed her journal and placed it on the checkered picnic blanket.

"And you're already fully booked for next summer." Logan snuggled up to Caitlyn and kissed her neck. "Didn't I tell you, Mrs. Beckett, the best is yet to come?"

A tear trickled down her cheek. She looked up at the cloudless blue sky, unable to respond. How quickly kisses with Logan became second nature. Of course, for her and Logan, everything seemed to happen quickly.

Following their brief engagement and wedding, there'd been no time for a honeymoon. As soon as she and Henry had moved into Logan's house, Caitlyn had gone to work on her to-do list. Turning Last Dollar into an all-inclusive barrel racing camp had been Logan's brilliant idea. The camp would offer week-long stays hosting girls from all over the country during June, July and August. The rest of the year, the home would provide overnight accommodations to people interested in rescuing a dog from Logan's organization. In addition, lodging was available to Beckett's Canine Training.

"Hey, no tears allowed on Henry's birthday."

The entire family, along with many friends from town, gathered to celebrate Henry's big day. The sound of his laughter while skipping stones across the pond with his cousins brought warmth to her heart. Since the day Logan had officially adopted Henry, her son had worn an unrelenting smile. She loved seeing him this way.

"Mom! Dad! Look!" Henry pointed to the water.

Caitlyn looked up at Henry, but the sun's glare prevented her from seeing what had caught his attention in the pond.

Cooper barked at the commotion.

"Let's go see." Logan jumped up and extended his hand to help Caitlyn to her feet.

Standing at the water's edge, alongside Logan, Jake, Olivia, Cody and the children, Caitlyn placed her palm to her heart. It was Donald. She was gliding across the glistening water with eight fuzzy ducklings trailing behind.

Logan placed his arm around Caitlyn and pulled her close. "The best is yet to come," he whispered into her ear.

"This is the best birthday ever!" Henry whooped. "Donald isn't alone anymore. She has a family now—just like me."

Caitlyn smiled. She'd never kept a secret from Logan, but she wanted to share the news with him privately, at home later. Earlier in the week, during her doctor's appointment with Olivia, she'd shared some symptoms she'd been experiencing. Olivia had done a few tests, and before Henry's party had started, had texted with the results. Caitlyn was six weeks pregnant. Logan was right. Sometimes the unexpected events in life made the greatest memories.

Caitlyn whispered back into Logan's ear, "I think you're right. The best is yet to come."

* * * * *

If you liked this story from Jill Weatherholt,
check out her previous Love Inspired books:

Searching for Home
A Dream of Family
A Home for Her Daughter
Their Inseparable Bond

Available now from Love Inspired!
Find more great reads at
www.LoveInspired.com.

Dear Reader,

Thank you for joining me in Bluebell Canyon! It's been a joy to introduce you to fresh faces and places in town while revisiting familiar characters.

My stories often include a few of my own cherished memories and personal experiences. If you follow me on Instagram, you already know Donald.

Sometimes after reaching the end of a book, I realize I'm stronger than I think. While writing Caitlyn and Logan's story, instead of embracing Logan's belief that the future holds great things, I battled thoughts that the worst was yet to come. When I sat down to write, my mind would cloud with worries. The constant replay in my head was "I'm never going to finish this book."

One day, I recalled my mother's words. In her advanced stage of Alzheimer's, the day I received the Beckett Brothers' book contract, she said, "You can do it." Recalling her reassuring words, I reflected on the seven books I've written, each crafted with God's grace and the encouragement of my mother, I knew I could do it again.

I love to hear from readers. You can find me at jillweatherholt.com.

Blessings,
Jill